CW01163269

TRAFFIC OF A *Lie*

ANGELA NAGEL

Traffic of a Lie
Copyright © 2024 by Angela Nagel

All rights reserved. No part of this publication may be reproduced, distributed, or transmitted in any form or by any means, including photocopying, recording, or other electronic or mechanical methods, without the prior written permission of the author, except in the case of brief quotations embodied in critical reviews and certain other non-commercial uses permitted by copyright law.

tellwell

Tellwell Talent
www.tellwell.ca

ISBN
978-1-998482-06-1 (Hardcover)
978-1-998482-05-4 (Paperback)
978-1-998482-07-8 (eBook)

DEDICATION

WITH LOVE AND THANKS

To my mum for unknowingly inspiring me to write this book.
My husband, James, for your continued
support, confidence, and belief in me.
Paul, Melissa, and Cameron—my pride and joy.
Our friend Andy, for the continued friendship, wit, and
laughter with which you immeasurably fill our lives.
Barbara, Kim, Russell and Michaela—
for reading my raw manuscript.

TABLE OF CONTENTS

DEDICATION		iii
PROLOGUE		1
Chapter 1	Fatima – Then	6
Chapter 2	Yasmina – Then	10
Chapter 3	Yasmina – Then	15
Chapter 4	Yasmina – Then	29
Chapter 5	Alif – Then	37
Chapter 6	Alif – Then	43
Chapter 7	Yasmina – Then	54
Chapter 8	Khalif – Then	65
Chapter 9	Yasmina – Then	75
Chapter 10	Elsie – Then	87
Chapter 11	Elsie – Then	103
Chapter 12	Elsie - Then	111
Chapter 13	Grace – Then	122
Chapter 14	Elsie – Then	128
Chapter 15	Alif – Then	133
Chapter 16	Alif – Then	143
Chapter 17	Alif – Then	150
Chapter 18	Sabrina – Then	158

Chapter 19	Henrique – Then	164
Chapter 20	Malik – Then	172
Chapter 21	Adeline – Now	177
Chapter 22	Adeline – Now	182
Chapter 23	Adeline – Now	191
Chapter 24	Mother's Letter	200
Chapter 25	Six Months Later – Adeline - Now	215
EPILOGUE		218
AUTHOR'S NOTE		220
ABOUT THE AUTHOR		221

PROLOGUE

'And that concludes the reading of the will.'

Edward Wharton, a long-time associate of their mother, leaned back in the exquisitely carved, soft, dove-coloured leather chair, his fingers entwined. Pausing, he reached forward, gently closing the lid of his laptop, his bespoke cufflinks, a gift from the girls' mother several years before, clinking the side of the computer quietly as they connected. His final assignment, as specified by the girls' mother, was now fulfilled, and knowing that this would be his final affiliation with the family saddened him. The four of them were seated in the boardroom—Edward at the head, Adeline and Penelope on either side, their mother's solicitor, Caleb, at the far end.

Their mother had designed the boardroom with no expense spared. Its tastefully decorated classic tones complemented the bespoke oak carved twelve-seater table, which had been commissioned from an English master craftsman, and was surrounded by soft buck leather chairs in an oatmeal colour. Generally, it was a room of comfort to the two girls, a room where they had spent many contented hours over the years by their mother's side whilst she worked on her couture fashion business. But the room now had an air of austerity to it.

Silence filled the space momentarily, as the contents of the will were digested. 'What do you mean that concludes the reading of the will?' Penelope eventually exploded, thumping her fist on the table as if it were a gavel. 'This doesn't make sense.' Her voice was shrill, emanating indignation, anguish, and exasperation, all rolled into one, as she looked from Edward to Adeline, her head and eyes darting swiftly between the two of them, as if she were at a tennis match.

'I don't understand! What about Adeline? This is preposterous!' Penelope, umbrage squirrelling across her brows, glared accusingly at Edward, demanding answers.

Looking up, Adeline caught Edward's eye, weariness evident, a sadness seeming to flow from him, she thought. Edward, seated to her left, was immaculately presented as always, his crisp white shirt complementing his olive complexion. His dark hair, still thick and abundant, precisely clipped, had been a part of their lives for as long as she could remember. He was strong, dependable, fun. Without a father on the scene, Edward had been the only constant male figure the girls had ever known. While he didn't fill the fatherly role, per se, he provided a male perspective, a balance of opinions when needed. Never having had a family of his own, Edward had filled the void with Mother, Penelope, and Adeline—his adopted family. Edward's guidance, gentle and persuasive, always had their best interests at heart.

The girls had never questioned Edward's presence in their lives; he was just always there. Adeline sat still, her face ghostly white, the newly acquired knowledge rendering her mute whilst she tried to process the information just communicated. Her hammering chest was beating rapidly, rising, and falling with her increased heart rate; her breathing was ragged, her back ramrod straight. Why had Mother excluded her in the will? What did that mean? She didn't understand. Her mind failed to register the logistics, and she was bewildered. She had always been very close to her beloved mother. They had never had a falling out or harsh words.

Mother had been diagnosed with advanced ovarian cancer only eight short weeks before. Aggressive treatment offered the hope of extending her time on earth, but she had declined, opting, as she had put it, for quality time left instead of quantity. Both she and Penelope had been shattered by their mother's adamant refusal of treatment, frustrated with her reticence to even consider trialling the new treatments and opportunities that were being continually made available with the advancement of each new medical breakthrough. Her impassivity to their pleas made it look as if she had given up the will to live; her indifference was almost as if she was welcoming of an expiry date.

Adeline's mind wandered back. Mother's passive acceptance of her diagnosis had completely bewildered Penelope and her. Why wasn't she considering treatment, pursuing all available avenues to prolong her time here with them, her girls? They had obsessed over these questions, firing them at Edward one evening whilst visiting him in the quaint cottage in which he lived on the estate, feeling crushed after yet another futile conversation with Mother.

'I just don't understand her reasoning. I would have thought she'd do everything she possibly could to extend her life, her time here with us,' lamented Penelope, her voice breaking with the onslaught of tears, her bottom lip quivering, matching the emotion of her voice. Bringing Penelope into a hug, her distress escalating, Adeline had held her tightly, patting her back soothingly; after some minutes her convulsions calmed down. Edward, infallibly dependable, the person they'd always turned to, had looked across at Adeline, over Penelope's downcast head, he himself looking visibly grave at the reality of the girls' situation. His voice was throaty, barely more than a whisper, when he said, 'It is not for you to judge or condemn, girls.'

He had paused then, a fleeting look of something Adeline couldn't quite put her finger on seeming to cross his eyes, his brow furrowed. 'But simply to support and respect your mother's decision.' Pausing again, he had taken a deep breath in, holding it long before expelling. There had been a sadness about him.

'Embrace what little time you have left together, for regret is a destructive demon,' he'd said. Hearing his words, Penelope had lifted her head and the two girls had looked at him, the sense of his words resonating. And so, they'd done just that.

Saying goodbye to a loved one is never easy. Heartbreaking in the wistful reminiscing of good times shared, shattering with the future knowledge that there will be no more memories to make. Whether you know death is imminent or whether it's by the cruel twist of fate, sudden and without warning, one can never be prepared for the brevity of the situation. Whilst the family had cherished the past eight weeks as much as possible, it had also been filled with much sadness and tears, not enough time to say all that they needed to be said, and the inevitable final heart-wrenching goodbye. *Nothing but memories were left now*, Adeline had thought as her mother had taken her last, rasping breath. Precious memories. Mother hadn't discussed the contents of her will with them, and neither she nor Penelope had ever asked any questions. Edward's reading of the will, delivered methodically, and perhaps a smidgeon nervously, she now reflected, had completely and undeniably knocked her off her axis; her world suddenly felt unbalanced.

The beginnings of a headache probed sharply at her temples; her mind was a tangled quagmire of disbelief, confusion, and incomprehension. Edward, slowly and with purpose, withdrew an envelope from within the leather-bound wallet before him, and passed it across the polished table surface to Adeline. 'Your mother's instructions were to hand this letter to you at the end of the reading of the will. To be read in private by you.' Edward's hand hovered in the space between Adeline and him, the envelope between them, Adeline frozen to the spot, hesitating, unable or reluctant to reach out and accept it, her tension palpable. For some unknown reason—gut instinct, intuition, or whatever— something told her that this letter would change everything. Edward sighed resignedly, mist clouding his eyes. He placed the envelope down gently on the table in front of her. Finally, Adeline expelled a long-held breath, her shaking hand hovering over the envelope before her. Touching it, acknowledging it, would change everything. Edward's quiet voice broke into her reverie: 'Now, if you ladies will excuse me, I'll bid you farewell.

CHAPTER 1

Fatima - Then

The sun's harsh rays beat down, its intensity a juxtaposition to the beauty of the ripened fruit crop below, the tree branches swayed in the hot breeze, the leaves ebbing and flowing like waves on the ocean reaching for the rays above. Fatima's husband, Khalif, surveyed his land before him, eyes squinting against the bold glare. He gratefully gulped down the glass of iced lemon water she handed him. Fatima watched the escaped droplets falling from either side of his mouth.

'A good crop.' He was a man of few words, stating facts as needed. Fatima looked at her husband, at his wizened body, moulded by years of hard physical toil. After thirty years of marriage, they had a comfort between them that didn't need a barrage of words.

'That it is,' she responded, not adding the obvious: that it was about time after the failures of the crops over the past five years.

Life on the land there wasn't for the faint-hearted, dealing as it did with elements beyond one's control. Drought was a constant battle, having ravaged the land more often than not. She peered into the distance. The Atlas Mountains, over two kilometres away, were hazy in their magnificence. Their family farm was generational, their small parcel of land located in the Sjel Balhro region located on the desert side of the mountains, the demographics dry and hot as opposed to the other side, where the temperatures were cooler, the rainfall higher. This region had primarily been of a nomadic existence due to its harsh conditions, but steadily more people were settling on a permanent basis, needing stability. Resilience and stoicism were requisites to survival here in this harsh landscape, Fatima reflected. Looking toward the house, she peered appreciatively across their simplistic back garden, it's design tidy and minimalist. Her eyes draw to the succulent garden featured along the northern fence line, it brimming with an abundance of colorful plants, sustainable and thriving under the warm climate. A stone laid garden path meanders toward the back verandah of the house, its route snaking around several fig and orange trees, each fecund with a flourish of deliciously ripened fruit. She spied their daughter, Yasmina, who was seventeen and beautiful, as she appeared at the doorway, leaning against the frame, her nose in a book. Without hesitation, Fatima called out across the short distance to the house. 'Please put the potatoes on Yasmina. I need to help Pappa for a while yet before prayer time.'

A moment elapsed, then without looking up from her book, Yasmina's voice, sanguine, 'Mamma, may I please finish reading this chapter?' Her tone rose questioningly at the end of her sentence, her stance unmoving, so absorbed was she in her book. It was a rhetorical question, as Fatima knew it was her daughter's intention to finish the chapter regardless.

'Yasmina, please. Do so now or they will not be ready in time for supper,' Fatima called out again, exasperated. Sighing, she thought about her daughter. Her education had unfortunately been sporadic and poor, though her thirst for knowledge had been evident at a young age. She had a brilliant mind, destined for greatness, denied by demographics. Fatima's brother, Brahim, would save old newspapers, booklets, and magazines, irrelevant of how tattered and torn the pages, any reading matter that he could retrieve, so readily disposed of by the travellers he met passing through his hometown, a small township of Habral, the travellers on their way to Romogdor. Living in the scenic Sjrabol Valley, located on the ancient caravan route where camels would once carry goods from Africa through the area on their way to the port, Brahim enjoyed interacting with the tourists. Dressing in traditional attire with his faithful camel Casablanca by his side, he made a meagre income, just enough to eat and have a roof over his head, posing for photos, the tourists lapping up the perceived authenticity of their visit and embracing the nostalgia and ways of times past. He would ask them for any reading paraphernalia, happily relieving them of extra baggage then passing them on to Fatima. She ensured she was discreet in receiving the reading paraphernalia, respectful of Khalif's views. Khalif was staunch, entrenched in the old ways, patriarchal. Women were considered the custodians and caretakers of the household, an education unnecessary. Men were the providers. Female oppression was still prevalent in these regions. Khalif didn't imbue his thoughts in a denigratory manner, but more so, factual, it was just so and Fatima was accepting of these circumstances.

But how could she deny such an intelligent mind in Yasmina, her daughter's insatiable appetite for knowledge, wanting to know more about the world around her? Was that so wrong? Squinting, Fatima folded her arm across her eyes, blocking out the sunlight, peering across the yard.

'Of course, Mamma,' Yasmina said, her soft voice disappearing back into the house. Fatima's thoughts were brought back to the present as she heard the local mosque's call to prayer peeling across the region. The sound, beckoning, welcoming, was one of which she never tired, even though she heard it five times a day. She saw Khalif donning his tools, heading to the prayer room at the back of the lean-to, his gait slow, his limp becoming more and more evident each passing day. He never complained but Fatima knew his arthritis was paining him significantly. The natural herbal supplements didn't seem to provide the level of relief that his pain dictated.

CHAPTER 2

Yasmina – Then

Peeling the potatoes, humming a tune contentedly, Yasmina set about preparing the *maakouda batata*, a family favourite, a recipe she'd learnt from her mother at an early age. She would serve them as a side dish alongside the tomato and olive tajine she'd prepared earlier in the day. She had helped prepare the family meals for as long as she could remember. Sighing dreamily, she thought about the contented hours she'd spent in this very kitchen, her mother passionate about cooking, passing on her zest and enthusiasm for all variety of dishes. Her mamma particularly liked international cuisine, sparking all manner of conversations about other countries that Yasmina had read about, their traditions, geography, education . . . the list was endless. Oh, how they'd talked and laughed as they'd rolled, patted, proofed, shaped, whisked, measured, and beat the doughs and ingredients. Pappa had often shaken his head, pretending they were both crazy but discreetly loving the laughter and chatter of his two 'girls'. The potatoes on the stove, Yasmina set about setting the wooden table located against the wall in their tiny kitchen, the wood worn from its use over the past few generations. The kitchen table . . . the hub of any family. How interesting if this table could talk, she mused—the stories it could tell, the conversations it had heard over the years. It would be marvellous! *An interesting thought, a talking table.* She smiled broadly to herself. Her daydreaming was interrupted by Karim, her ten-year-old brother, as he bounded into the room, his words of excitement tumbling out over themselves. He couldn't expel his news quickly enough. Always an abundance of energy and exuberance. 'Yassy, Yassy,' he squealed. 'Shasta has birthed her kittens, eight of them.' His excitement was infectious.

'Really?' Eyebrows raised, lips upturned, Yasmina joined in with her brother's enthusiasm. 'Come, come, Yassy, come and see!' Karim's eagerness was contagious, his face brightly lit. Putting down the dishcloth she was holding, Yasmina skipped out after her brother, and both headed a distance to the ramshackle barn down by the farther paddock to see the newest additions to the family. 'Race you,' Yasmina said and bolted off at a speed as they exited the lean-to attached to the back of the house, turning her head as she called out to Karim. Not to be outdone by his sister, Karim took off after her, laughing, seconds behind. 'Not fair, Yassy, you had a head start.' He laughed as he gained on her, the distance between them lessening. Reaching the barn, both breathless, leaning over and puffing heavily, they quietened, not wanting to scare Shasta.

'You brave, brave girl, Shasta,' murmured Yasmina half an hour later, crouching beside the feline, caressing her head and behind the ears as the cat so enjoyed. Obviously exhausted from her efforts, the mother cat lay quietly, seemingly enjoying the massage bestowed lovingly on her by Yasmina. The tiny kittens made mewling noises, blindly searching for the comfort and nourishment of their mother's teats, squirming over each other.

'Can I pick one up, Yassy? I want to cuddle them all—they are so cute,' enquired Karim, excitedly reaching forward.

'I would advise against it.' The pronouncement startled them both. Yasmina and Karim turned their heads in the direction of the deep, gentle voice. 'It's best to resist handling them until their eyes are open—generally a week. Their mamma will be very protective of her new family and may not be comfortable with you handling them, even possibly causing her to reject the kittens.'

'Oh, no, Karim, please don't touch them. We don't want to upset Shasta,' Yasmina interjected, horrified at the thought of Shasta rejecting any of her beautiful babies, before suddenly realizing she didn't know this stranger who had joined them in their barn. Neither she nor Karim had heard him enter, so engrossed had they been in Shasta and her new family. The stranger, straightening up from his bent-over position, proffered his hand. 'Alif, my apologies for my intrusion. I was on the road behind your barn here completing some soil test studies and was intrigued by the excitement of voices.'

Not realizing their excitement had been that loud, Yasmina said, 'Oh, I guess we did get carried away here.... What brings you to this region? We don't get many visitors apart from locals through here.' She paused. There was something vaguely familiar about this man, she thought, unable to quite put her finger on it. The handsome stranger responded, 'I'm an environmental agriculturist,' nodding his head at the girl.

'A what?' Karim asked, frowning.

'It's someone who studies the issues, impacts and solutions to agronomic and horticulturalist production,' Yasmina blurted forth without thinking. Blushing she had looked down, surprised at the ease of her forthrightness with this stranger. Suitably impressed, Alif, eyebrows raised and looking over the head of Karim at the young lady before him, noted the pink tinge creeping over her cheeks, spreading down her neck, the blush and downward lashes suggesting an innocent modesty about her. Interrupting, Karim said, his pride obvious, 'My sister is very intelligent.' He emphasised the word *very*.

'She doesn't go to school anymore because girls don't get properly educated. They have to learn the ways to run a home, but Mamma says that's degrotry against women.'

Alif smiled, amused at the boy's mispronunciation of 'derogatory.'

'She says girls have as much right to be educated and are just as clever and capable as men,' Karim said, now standing, hands on hips, his stance rigid to get his point of view across. 'She says King Amine is to blame for oppressing women; he should do a lot more to change the rules!'

His arms were now crossed against his chest as if to reaffirm his stance on the subject. Horrified at the verbal diatribe, but full of love for his unconditional support of her, Yasmina playfully grabbed hold of her brother and held him in a loose headlock, a hand over his mouth to stop anymore of his forth-righteousness. Karim struggled to squirm his way free. Yasmina leaned toward his ear. 'Thank you, Karim. . . . Now please go back to the house.' And as an afterthought, she added, 'And do not mention to Mamma and Pappa our stranger's visit.' She wasn't sure why she'd added this last bit, but thinking she needed some time to process what was going on, Yasmina released her brother from his headlock, placing her hands gently on his shoulders instead. Frowning at her, Karim waved enthusiastically at Alif as he departed. 'Ma'a al-ssalamah', *goodbye* he said, and with a quick gentle tickle behind Shasta's ears he was gone.

A smile spread across Alif's face, the obvious closeness and affection between brother and sister warming him. 'A most genuine young man, refreshingly speaking his honesty.'

'I will not apologise for my brother's words for he speaks the thoughts of Mamma and me. The oppression of women is a disgrace,' blurted Yasmina. Gasping, she thought, *Why am I stating this? I'm as bad as Karim. What has overcome the pair of us?* She clutched her mouth, her self-consciousness evident. Alif was fascinated by this girl before him. He reached across and gently took her hand from her mouth. 'I agree with you.'

Stunned, Yasmina stared at the stranger standing before her, absorbing the context and simplicity of those four words—*I agree with you*. She'd had to suppress the intensity of her emotions her whole life about the unfairness of having been born female, the injustices women faced in an outdated patriarchal male-dominated system. Something stirred within her, primal.

CHAPTER 3

Yasmina – Then

Two months had passed since the chance encounter in the barn with Alif. They had met up another three times since then. Yasmina's heart skips with joy, a fluttering dance of elation pounding in her chest, exultant, the details of each rendezvous engraved in her mind. She couldn't stop thinking about Alif, their chance encounter dominating her every waking thought as well as creeping into her night dreams. Karim hadn't mentioned the encounter with this stranger to their parents as she had requested, though his mind was preoccupied with the arrival of the kittens, and he spent every spare moment he had in the barn with them. 'They are so cute,' he exuded over supper one night, announcing and reciting the names of each of them, regaling the four of them as they sat around the dinner table enjoying their evening meal, with all the kittens' quirky little antics and personalities. Yasmina welcomed Karim's dominance over the dinnertime discussions, relieving her from having to contribute to the conversation. His constant chatter allowed her to remain immersed in her own thoughts, the inkling that she had seen Alif's profile somewhere before still vague in the recesses of her mind. After their last rendezvous ... *date*, she tingles at the thought, the mere suggestion of the word date inciting a heady elixir of excitement within her, Alif had asked if he could see Yasmina again—in another week's time, he'd explained, when he would be re-visiting this region.

He had vocalised how impressed he had been with Yasmina's explanation of his career choice and her equal interest and knowledge about the workings of the land. He'd said he found intelligence attractive. Yasmina had been flattered by his admission, a statement that she'd never heard before. No one apart from her own family had ever called her intelligent. Her and Alif's conversations were interesting, challenging, vibrant, and varied; their discussions covered a range of topics particularly relevant to farming in their region regarding the difficulties and variables encountered—with rainfall, or, more precisely, lack thereof, a known major problem. 'We cannot change the weather patterns,' Alif said, stating the obvious. 'But we can farm smarter and more sustainably.' He had said this one day during one of their liaisons, gently stroking the back of Yasmina's head, his fingers gently caressing her hair. She had soaked up every word he'd uttered, hung onto them, totally enamoured by this man.

Purposely, she hadn't shared her news about Alif with her parents, wanting to explore and savour whatever it was that was developing between them, not wanting to have to deal with prying parental questions, endeavouring to catalogue her own feelings into some kind of context. These feelings had crept up on her in the most improbable of circumstances and had taken her completely by surprise. This connection they seemed to share was all new to her, and something she felt she needed to process on her own, substantiate this wasn't some fantasy she was imagining. Her interaction with males had been extremely limited up until this point. She'd never met anyone remotely like Alif. Just the thought of him made her heart skip a beat, a feeling she realised she welcomed. This blanket of euphoria that had enveloped her was hers and hers alone at the present time. She savoured what she felt was a blossoming romance, their special trysts, their snatched moments together, and Alif completely consumed her mind.

Yasmina wasn't entirely oblivious to reality though, knowing in her heart that they heralded from completely different backgrounds. Perhaps it was serendipity though. Like two worlds colliding, they had randomly connected and had done so on what she felt was a deep level. Alif, with his tidy manicured nails, soft hands, custom-made shoes, and impeccable speech was not like her people. He asked many questions about her family and enjoyed hearing her anecdotes about life on the farm, her familial interactions, her normality—they seemed to intrigue him. When she'd ask Alif about his family, eager to know as much as she could about this man that had captured her heart, he was reserved, sharing only a few snippets, which she found disappointing, wanting to know everything about him, but learning very little. He always deflected the conversation back to Yasmina and her family. But she respected his privacy. He must have his reasons, she'd determined.

'Isn't that right, Yassy?' Karim's voice broke through her reverie, his forehead punctuated in a crinkled frown, confused by his sisters newfound dreamy demeanour of late. She was standing at the kitchen sink washing the dishes after another enjoyable and relaxed family evening.

'Mmm, yes, Karim,' she answered absent-mindly, having no idea what she was agreeing to, her thoughts with Alif. She couldn't contain the smile spreading across her face. She felt giddy with excitement, knowing this Saturday she was meeting up with Alif, her memory readily conjuring up the image of his strong jawline, dimpled chin, and perfectly aligned pearly white teeth, her mind devouring the vision like an intoxicating tonic. She suddenly realises the incessant background hum of Karim's chatter has quietenend, drawing her thoughts back to the present ... she's obviously missed something? 'Yassie, your head is in the clouds again', Karim's laughter tinkled through the air, a mischievious connotation attached to the lightness in his voice. 'Are you thinking about Alif again', emphasizing Alif loudly. 'Alif and Yassie, sitting in a tree K.I.S.S.I.N.G.' He leans across Yasmina, a playful smirk planted over his face. Dunking his hands into the kitchen sink, he flicks a spray of soapy suds through her hair before running away laughing, chants of 'you can't catch me', ringing through the kitchen. 'Karim', she shrieked, trying to grab hold of her brother, grasping at thin air instead! Shaking the suds from her hair, she bounds after her brother, needing to remind him to please not mention Alif's name out loud as he had just done so in case Mamma and Pappa overheard, not to mention payback for the suds in her hair!

The following Saturday dawned hot. Yasmina's house was like a sauna, with not even a breath of air to stir the atmosphere from its oppressiveness. Even the birds seemed to be flat, the air quiet from any birdsong, as they saved their energy, sitting quietly in the trees. She was meeting Alif later that morning. Karim had ventured off to the goat shed; he would be there for hours cleaning it out and messing about with the goats. Circumstances couldn't have worked out more favourably for Yasmina. She didn't need to fabricate a story to her parents about where she was going or figure out how to extricate herself to slip away to meet Alif for their rendezvous as Mamma and Pappa had gone to visit the neighbours, Yasmina's Aunt Sabrina and her second cousin Malik. They had invited her to join them and, recalling the invitation, a shudder of dread shimmied down her back. When they'd mentioned it, she'd declined, feigning that she instead wanted to devote the morning to cleaning the house. It was a lame excuse and certainly not what she would consider an enjoyable way to spend a morning; however, her parents seemed to accept her excuse with Mamma leaving instructions of a few household chores she wanted completed.

Even if she hadn't been meeting Alif, the thought of visiting Aunt Sabrina and her horridly, obnoxious son Malik filled her with dread. Aunt Sabrina was a complicated woman, as if she were two personalities rolled into one. You never knew which personality you were going to get with her. She could be all sweet and charming one moment and then, without warning, she could be nasty and vindictive. It was exhausting and confusing. Yasmina paused from her dusting, her mind wandering, the synapses of memory emitting a vile taste in her brain. She distinctly recalled one day several years before when she, Pappa and Karim had been visiting Aunt Sabrina. Mamma had been unwell, unable to join them. The occasion had been for Aunt Sabrina's birthday, and as soon as they had arrived the children were relegated to stay outdoors for the afternoon. *Children should be seen but not heard.* Aunt Sabrina had laughed long and hard as she ushered the three of them outside without even as much as a cold drink to appease the heat. It had been a stifling hot day. Malik was grumpy at not being allowed to go into the house. He had beckoned Karim and Yasmina to follow him down to the creek that ran through their property. The water in the creek had long ceased to flow; the creek bed was parched, cracked, dry earth. They had followed him, not having anything else to do with themselves.

Malik had stopped still, suddenly, Karim immediately behind him, bumping into his back. Malik had turned around abruptly. 'Piss off, you idiot!' he'd bellowed, pushing Karim, who was half Malik's size, forcefully, propelling him backward. Karim had landed heavily on his back, his head hitting the ground with a loud thud. Yasmina had instantly kneeled beside her brother, checking him over before gently helping him upright, Karim desperately trying to hold the tears at bay that threatened to erupt, obviously hurting from the fall. Malik, indifferent to their plight and sighting a lizard that was sunning itself, positioned half in and half out of one of the deep creek bed cracks, bent over it and pulled the innocent creature's tail hard, dislodging the sleeping reptile. Holding the helpless lizard high in front of him, its tail pinched firmly between his dirty, stubby fingers, he had started vigorously swinging it around and around, laughing menacingly, a guttural sound, evil and dirty, spewing from his mouth. A wide smile had spread across his cheeks, his toothless grin matching the malevolent glint in his eyes; his behaviour was despicably cruel, as one by one he slowly pulled on the helpless lizard's legs, dislocating each in turn before cracking the poor mangled creature's back. The lizard dangled, its body broken.

Horrified at his torturous behaviour toward this poor, innocent creature, Yasmina had screamed at him to stop. 'Oh, yeah, you gonna make me?' he'd taunted. 'Poor little lizard.' He'd held it up, swaying it from side to side. 'Here, if it means so much to you, have it.' And with that, he'd smashed it into Yasmina's face, its head landing in her opened mouth as she'd screamed in horror.

Yasmina had grabbed Karim's hand and the two of them had started running from Malik as fast as their legs would carry them, wishing to put as much distance between them and him. They'd raced back to the house, Malik's bullying voice distancing behind them in the hot air. Puffing loudly from their exertion, they'd rounded the corner of the house, seeing the bench seat under the kitchen window, and parked themselves on it, heaving and panting, trying to catch their breath.

The kitchen window was open. Sharpening their ears, they could hear Aunt Sabrina's voice grating through the airwaves. Her tone was low and sharp. 'That bitch, Fatima... I wouldn't trust her word any more than I'd trust the sun to rise in the evening. She is a hypocrite,' her voice hissed. 'And what's more, she owes me. Under no circumstances will I let her lay any claim to what is rightfully mine!'

Yasmina couldn't make any sense of what Aunt Sabrina was going on about, but by the nasty tone of her voice she knew she was stirring trouble again. Pappa had said before that she had a jealous streak and that lies came easily to her. Karim and Yasmina strained their ears, listening intently. Then Pappa's voice, low and quiet, reached their ears: 'This has to stop, Sabrina. Your nastiness, your lies. You are delusional.'

Snapping back to the present, not wishing to dampen her good mood by thinking about Aunt Sabrina or Malik, Yasmina focused on working through her list of household chores. Humming a lullaby tune to herself, she quickly finished dusting the console table, ensuring she'd put the ornaments each back in their correct position, knowing Mamma liked everything to be just right, so proud was she of their home. Once finished, she changed into her favourite dress, light blue with tiny white flowers on it. It had been Mamma's dress when she was her age and she had told Yasmina the story of how she'd worn it the day she'd met Pappa and how it held a special place in her heart. Yasmina loved hearing the story of how they met and so by association the dress was now also special to her. Now, years later, somewhat worn, it draped easily over her body, hugging her curves in all the right places. Feeling pretty, she skipped out the back door, her excitement heightened at the thought of meeting Alif.

'So, what occupation would you choose if you could be anything, me lady?' Alif asked. He imitated an English accent—to the best of his ability, a little joke between the two of them after she'd read *Pride and Prejudice,* the tattered book given to her from her Uncle Brahim, and now Yasmina was in awe of anything English. They were at their secret little meeting place, having been seeing each other for several months by then, and having claimed this little spot, located in an olive grove not far from her home, conveniently accessible for Yasmina to cycle to and from easily on her rickety old bike without raising any suspicions, as their own. The gnarled tree branches were knotted together, unkempt, making a canopy, the two of them deeming it as perfect, and they'd laid their picnic blanket under it.

Conversation was easy between them, and they talked about subjects that ranged from topical to challenging, inquisitive and philanthropic, as much as their banter was playful and fun.

'Oh. you do jest me, Lord,' Yasmina had laughingly replied, gently rubbing Alif's bare arm, which lay across her thigh.

'No jest, I assure you, me dear,' he'd said, piling on the thick English accent. 'Your wish is my desire.' Playfully, he'd risen up from the picnic rug to a standing position, clipping the side of his head on a low lying branch as he did so. Unperturbed, he bent over, one hand placed in the small of his back, the other effusively waving in front of him, flourishing an elegant bow, his broad smile accentuating his dimples. She had laughed, an easy energy between them.

'Mmmmm,' Yasmina had said, nibbling on the inside of her cheek, a habit when she was thinking, contemplating momentarily. 'Well, then, that's easy. Without question I would be a human rights campaigner,' she'd answered Alif's question, her voice light, watching him as he wriggled himself back down onto the rug beside her.

She hoisted herself up, leaning on her elbow, facing Alif, suddenly feeling serious at the thought of having a choice of career. No one had ever asked her that question.

'If I had this platform I would relish the opportunity, devoting my time to helping those in need, advocating change, giving the voiceless a voice.' She felt her eyes lighting up, her voice lilting melodiously, the very thought of having a choice warming. Alif had looked at her, a deep sincerity in his eyes, as he entwined his fingers through hers.

'My beautiful Yasmina, so vivacious, selfless, and always so thoughtful of others; such admirable qualities,' he'd said. A tender quietness had settled between them, the faint rustling of the tree leaves the only sound intervening.

'And you, me lord, what would be your goal in life, aside from the commendable environmental work you already do?' Yasmina had broken in, her voice sounding funny, as if she had a plum in her mouth, her parlance that of a posh accent. Alif had responded without hesitation, his own voice light with the sounds of laughter. 'That is an easy one. . . . I'd sail the seas, captain of my own ship, navigator of my own destiny,' he'd bantered, adopting a pirate's voice.

'We'd sail away together, you and I, aye, aye,' his eyes bright with undisguised merriment, 'exploring the world, conquering new horizons,' he'd quipped.

'That does sound mighty adventurous, me lord, particularly given that I've never sighted the ocean, let alone been on or in it,' she'd retorted, running her fingers down his arm, then entangling their palms together again, laughing, her mind conjuring up images she'd seen of savage seas when she'd read *Moby Dick*. They had both laughed, rolling back, relishing the easy lightheartedness of each other's company. Lying next to Alif, looking upward at the dappled sun as it twinkled through the leaves of the olive tree, Yasmina felt like they were in their own little bubble of heaven. She wished she could harvest this moment in time, the two of them, alone, together.

A cloud passed overhead, momentarily dampening the dappled sunlight. A quietness had then settled between them, each anchored in their own thoughts, her's sinking into her mood like an uninvited guest, suddenly sitting heavy, as if they were locked in a cavernous pit, buried deep within her soul. Hope, expectation and anticipation all rolled into one tight bundle. Yasmina all of a sudden wanted infinitely more than what she had ever dared to dream. Alif had awakened a craving within her, a craving filled with desire, of wanting to grow, live, experience, and embrace so much more in life, more than she'd ever thought possible—a yearning, she realised, that had lain dormant in the depths of her soul for years. She swallowed hard; the futility of her situation having lodged like an unwelcome lump in her throat. A ripple of frustration paired with disappointment grumbled through her veins. 'Anyway,' she said, an air of resignation escaping her lips, 'dreaming is all well and good.' She said this more to herself than to Alif.

Pausing, she gently flicked away a tiny black ant that had laboured its way onto their picnic blanket, the miniscule insect carrying a crumb bigger than itself, a crumb from the delicious *meskouta* orange cake Alif had brought. 'But as Jadda always tells me,' she said, turning to face Alif, 'I'm a dreamboat, and I should be grateful for what I have.' She imitated Grannie's deep, gravelly voice, a consequence from a lifetime of heavy smoking, her only joy in life, and she'd rebuked Yasmina when she'd implored her to give it up after reading about the effects of lung cancer. 'And not longing for a life that you cannot have.'

A deep sigh like a balloon about to burst escaped her lips. With a sudden flush of resentment, she felt an anger and annoyance toward the patriarchal society she had been brought up in. These dispiriting thoughts had been building, gaining momentum, flooding her mindset of late. Alif, wordless, took her palm to his lips, kissing it tenderly, a deep frown burrowed across his brow. They lay there together, quiet, side by side, languishing, not moving, their bodies cushioned on the most beautiful rug she'd ever seen, which Alif had brought along for their picnic. It was luxuriously quilted, exquisite in its glory of colours, each individual embroidery stitch unassuming on its own, but collectively a picture of beauty, a woman silhouetted against a blazing sunset of vibrant reds, pinks, oranges, and golden hues, each stitch tiny and delicately needled through the fabric. Alif said his mother had handstitched it but didn't elaborate, his eyes seeming to glaze over. *She must have had the patience of a saint to create this magnificent artwork*, Yasmina thought, caressing the silk softly between her fingers.

The leaves of the olive branches above them rustled in the gentle breeze, swaying and shimmering in the late afternoon's bask of golden rays, with only the gentle sounds of nature cajoling in the background. A dog started to bark in the distance, breaking into their silence, its pitch and volume escalating, rapid with excitement. *It had probably found a rabbit or some such creature to pursue*, Yasmina thought.

Alif shifted his body onto his side, facing her. She stroked her thumb across his hand as he leaned in to her, whispering, his soft lips against her ear: 'Never let your dreams be dampened, Yasmina, for without dreams we have nothing.' His voice was raspy with emotion. He kissed the palm of her hand again and again, his lips lingering against her skin. The delicate kisses tingled, soft, the warmth of his breath a kindling flame, comforting, filling her from within. Suddenly, feeling awkward, she had a fleeting unwelcome thought: *It is easy for Alif to utter these words, he is not shackled to the system the way I am.* Cross with herself for allowing such thoughts, she banished them as quickly as they had entered her head. Alif fidgeted before sitting upright, as if needing to fill the quiet space with movement. He lifted the ornate glass carafe, its design decadent, elegant, whence an ice bucket rested, the bucket sitting on the corner of the exquisite silken picnic blanket, and poured them both a mint tea. She noted the tinkling sound of the liquid splashing into the matching glasses—gentle, pretty, as it flowed from the decadent design of the carafe; Alif handed her the glass.

A butterfly flitted about, landing on Yasmina's knee, its delicate wings fluttering, an iridescent blue, outlined in black as if framing its beauty into a contained area. It wasn't stationary for long, flitting and fluttering all around them, its schedule busy, as if it had places to go, things to do. No time to sit still.

'Do you know, Alif,' Yasmina began, a butterfly fact she'd recently read about coming to mind, 'that butterflies don't fly when it rains because the raindrops can damage their wings? They rest and wait it out. It's self-preservation.'

Alif's head dropped to one side, his lopsided smile easing into a shy grin. He was humble, yes, *he knew that—she could tell—*his eyes said as much without words, but he obviously didn't wish to steal her moment to shine.

'My Habiba,' he said, and smiled, his rich voice melting her heart every time. 'The butterfly is a beautiful creature of wisdom. He knows it's OK to rest during the storms of life, for he knows the storm will pass and he will fly again afterward.' Alif straightened his head, his brow creasing with deep furrows again. *He really must stop frowning like that,* Yasmina thought momentarily, *He'll age his looks, or if the wind changes . . .* her mind went briefly off on a tangent, butterfly facts aside. Shaking her head as if it would dispel her errant thoughts, she refocused, ingesting Alif's words of butterfly wisdom, their taste churning and chewing around like tumbleweed inside her head; she didn't care to savour them. Her frustration had been steadily escalating these past weeks regarding the outdated patriarchal system of her country. It was a system that needed urgent overhauling, conducive to a more modern structure. None of it sat well on her scales of fairness agenda. *The way change moves forward in this country,* she thought exasperatedly, *I'll be old and grey before* it *happens, if it ever happens,* her truculent thoughts deepening. She flicked the ant that had crawled onto her leg away with a vengeance, feeling conflicted from so many emotions.

'Yasmina.' Alif's voice registered beside her, gentle, as she realised, she was simply lying there staring into the distance.

'No, Alif, I don't want to wait,' she babbled as if he's been privy to all her convoluted thoughts, the wretchedness of her situation propelling waves of hysteria into her voice. 'Nothing will change.' She picked at an unripened olive that had fallen into her lap, discarded from its place in the tree, suddenly overwhelmed by disparity. She drew in her breath long and hard, her stomach a twisted knot of nerves, 'I want to be free to make my own choices.' She heard the sharpness of her voice, then paused, waiting for Alif to respond. . . . But he didn't. He was devoid of words, his gaze reflective of deep thought.

The dog's barking reached their ears again, closer, its frenzied sound diminishing the consistent little voice whispering inside her head. They hauled themselves upright, their picnic finished, and went in search of the dog in case it needed help.

CHAPTER 4

Yasmina – Then

She sat still, staring out of her bedroom window. Sunrise. Yasmina's favourite part of the day. The glorious sun's rays reached out across the land, like tentacles spreading, expanding gloriously, basking the land below in a hallowed glow, a magnificent sight before her. A new day. The simple logistics of time and its precious gift wove through her mind, the beautiful thought of each new day promising the opportunity of new beginnings; yesterday was gone, non-retrievable, tomorrow was not promised.

The daily morning ritualistic sounds of the household echoed in the background. She could hear Mamma in the kitchen commandeering the ancient stovetop, simultaneously singing, her beautiful voice both hypnotic and soothing. The delectable aroma of Mamma's morning preparations of freshly baked bread, semolina pancakes, mint tea, goat's cheese, fried eggs and olives wafted through the house, tantalizing the family's tastebuds. It was a wholesome breakfast to sustain them all for the vigours of the morning's scheduled workload. Pappa and Karim were in the lean-to, noisily banging their workboots together, ensuring no surprises had crawled in during the night hours, before putting them on, busying for another day on the land, their easy banter and laughter discernible through her bedroom doorway. The tinkling sound of Mamma's bell rang out, the sound delicate, indicating that breakfast was ready. The bell was a gift from Pappa after Mamma had seen the idea on a movie some years back; Mamma deciding to summon them via the bell added class to their humble abode. They played along with Mamma's wish, ignoring the obvious that it was equally effective for her to call them verbally, so small was their abode.

Thoughts of Alif consumed her every waking moment these days. A cloudy haze ebbed and flowed, of having seen his face somewhere; it was never clarifying, but a feeling of familiarity was a constant at the back of her mind. Six months had passed since their first encounter. They met up as often as circumstances allowed, always in secret, always in the ramshackle back barn or in the olive grove. Both locations had become their little sanctuaries where they savoured their beautiful, snatched moments of privacy together. Conversation between them flowed easily and effortlessly. Alif listened with intent, constantly encouraging her opinions. He challenged her thoughts, supported her beliefs, and most importantly, valued her opinions. He made her feel validated. She felt her body heat up, her neck and face hot, as a creeping blush warmed her, thinking that conversation wasn't the only connection happening between them these days.

A beautiful, deep intimacy had developed between them. Closing her eyes, Yasmina felt her body tingle at the memory of his touch, his gentle and tantalising caresses. The very thought of Alif brought a fluttering to her stomach, like a kaleidoscope of butterflies. The memory tantalised her senses, teasingly, as she relived the memory of Alif's hands on her body, gentle and caressing, probing and seductive. Her blush rose again.

This pleasantness was short-lived though, as her mind spun backward, regurgitating their last rendezvous, only mere days before, tears pooling in her eyes at the recollection. She fiddled with the buttons down the front of her dress, her fingers clumsy with nerves, an errant thread catching, propelling the loose button across the floorspace, its brown colour camouflaging with the knot of the wood in the floorboard. Mamma's tinkling bell faded into the background as she sunk into the recollection.

It had been late afternoon, Pappa and Karim had been in the front paddock tending the goats, Mamma in the washhouse laundering. Yasmina was preparing the evening meal, hurriedly so, knowing Alif was waiting for her in the barn. Her heart aflutter, she'd swiftly prepared the meal of couscous accompanied with date lamb, and hurriedly set the table, deliberately choosing an easy meal plan that day. She'd run at speed, swift and nimble on her feet, an attribute of a childhood of physical toil, arriving within moments in the barn, breathless.

She'd burst through the barn doorway, immediately drinking in the delectable sight of the back of her beautiful Alif. She drew to a halt, just short of him, panting from the exertion of her run. Snaking her arms along his torso, she clasped them together around his front. He did a little wiggle of his derrière, rubbing against the front of her, sending her into shudders of delight. She eased her clutch, allowing him the space to turn around, still ensconced in her embrace. A giggle escaped her lips as she laid eyes on a long red rose clenched the breadth of his teeth; his face was a funny fixture, grinning and clenching. Taking the rose, she reached up on the tips of her toes to plant a kiss on his lips, the taste of his reciprocation heavenly. 'Thank you for my beautiful rose,' she murmured. 'Red, the colour of love.'

She yielded her head backward. Alif nuzzled his soft lips along her neck. 'A beautiful rose for my beautiful princess,' he said, the heat of his husky voice hot in her ear. They eased over to the bed of hay in the corner, Alif's mood suddenly playful and silly, his fingers running all over her, tickling effusively. Convulsing with laughter, squirming, Yasmina tried to push him away—so sensitive was she to being tickled. 'Stop, stop, stop,' she shrieked trying to catch her breath. 'Please,' she begged, her *please* long and drawn out, needing him to stop. 'You are making as much noise as a pack of laughing hyenas, Habiba', Alif said, laughing along with her. He had slowly withdrawn his hands; she had been grateful for the reprieve.

A quietness transcended between them. Yasmina fidgeted on the hay. It was prickly and spiky beneath her like a mass of brambles, the discomfort in sync with her erratic thoughts. Sitting upright, Alif leaned across, picking threads of hay from her tousled hair, an air of seriousness suddenly stamping out their silliness of moments prior. She turned sideways, cupping Alif's face, her hands gently placed on each cheek, caressing his stubbled skin, prickly beneath her fingertips, before placing a delicate kiss on the end of his nose. 'My darling Alif, my thoughts are consumed with my love for you,' she whispered, drinking in the scent of him. 'I cannot live without you, I see and feel your love everywhere, in everything, the beauty of a new day, the exquisiteness of a sunset, the resplendence of birdsong. My world is more beautiful because of your love.' She hears her words as they glide effortlessly from the tip of her tongue. She knows they sound a bit mushy, but it's her truth, flowing direct from her heart. Smiling, Alif, reached up and gently folded back a strand of her hair that had fallen across her face, twirling it around his finger. He leaned in close, his husky voice whispering to her, 'I know I have found my soulmate in you, my beautiful Habiba. Close your eyes, I have a little gift for you.'

She looked at him, surprised, but obeyed, slowly closing her eyes. She felt Alif's arms gently reaching around her neck. Inhaling deeply, she breathed in the scent of his maleness, his sandalwood and musk cologne mingling with a faint tinge of sweat, as she felt the sensation of a delicate chain settling in her decolletage. Opening her eyes, she looked downward, and lifted the delicate gold heart nestled elegantly between her breasts. Five little diamonds sparkled around the perimeter of the heart. Quietly gasping, she folded her fingers gently over the heart, caressing it. The beauty, the significance of the delicate piece of jewellery was more than anything she had ever seen. The gift was symbolic of their love for each other, the gold was also symbolic of another world foreign to her.

She was lost for words, her eyes suddenly misting over, thick like the early morning fog, her emotions overwhelming her. 'Habiba,' Alif said, as he took her hands in his, gently caressing them with his thumbs. She could feel the deep, dark depths of his eyes boring into her, focused with earnest, his brows furrowed with concern. 'Why the tears?' he asked. She bowed her head, her eyes drooping like a wilted flower, downcast, her swallowing exaggerated as she tried to navigate past the lump that sat like a massive boulder in her throat. The waves of sadness that she had tried to obliterate resurfaced, the tension settling tautly across her shoulders. Their fun and mirth from earlier were a smokescreen of their reality, she thought miserably. Unable to contain her emotions, the tears started to flow freely; raw, unadulterated emotions infiltrated every fibre of her being, her shoulders shuddered recklessly as her sobbing became uncontrollable.

She had been thinking about this moment for the past few weeks, thinking how she would explain her situation to Alif, dreading the thought of losing him. She felt Alif's strong arms envelope her, holding her close, her body moulding into his, as she convulsed uncontrollably, consumed with devastation of the news that she must share with him. Alif uttered soothing noises as he rubbed her back, trying to calm her anguish. They stayed like this for some time, fused together. Yasmina wished they could freeze this moment forever; she never wanted to let go. Eventually, a relative calm settled over her distraught state and her breathing regulated itself. Alif held her apart from him, looking searchingly into her eyes; the haunted look of her sadness stared back at him.

She gulped voluminously, taking in deep breaths, trying to compose herself in readiness to divulge her news. She began, her voice, barely audible. 'Alif . . . my beloved.' She took more deep breaths, shuddering, drawing out her sentence, her fingers shaking as she stroked his hair, needing to do something. 'My . . . my mind has been in undeniable turmoil these past few weeks. My heart brims with absolute unconditional love for you, my every waking moment is consumed by my thoughts for you.' She paused momentarily, hearing her voice breaking, so heavily laden with emotion. She continued, 'Even though I am young and haven't experienced being in love before, I have been blessed to grow up in a household where love is unconditional and in abundance. I understand what love is as I have seen it in the purest form from my parents.'

Her tears overflowed again, brimming like pools. She wiped them away with the back of her hand, trying to compose herself, sniffing loudly, the sound embarrassing. She drew in a long breath, deeply, before continuing. 'I believe our stars aligned that day in the barn . . . over the kittens.' Her lips twisted upward at the recollection of their first meeting. 'Such a random time and place, and yet our worlds came together in unusual circumstances. I truly believe it was our destiny.' She paused again, composing her words, as she straightened her back, a conviction of her words to come, feeling an urgency of needing to expunge them from her mouth. Alif sat unmoving, his full attention on her. 'I know we are from two very different worlds, Alif,' she said, looking directly at him. 'You don't speak of your background, and I don't question your reasons, but I can see you are refined in speech and manner, a man of integrity, an educated man, a man of quality, all qualities that I have fallen head over heels in love with.' She let the words linger, the atmosphere around them absorbing them.

She continued, 'This beautiful and generous gift of a necklace...' Her fingers plied the delicate gold chain hanging around her neck, 'is of worth and I will treasure it always.' She held the heart in her palm, relishing the love it endeared, before ploughing on. 'But... it is not a present my people would ever have the means to gift. My people are of simple means of the land, following in the ways and traditions of the generations before them. Nothing ever changes, nothing is ever questioned. Such an extravagant gift will be noticed, will incite questions.' Her words were now coming rapidly, tumbling out, tripping over each other.

She paused again, despondent, the weight of her words heavy. 'My heart is leaden.... I am eighteen next week and it has been arranged for me to marry Malik, our farming neighbour, my cousin.' Her words tumbled out fast, the urgency to expel the very mention of Malik from her tongue dire, the taste of his name repulsive and bitter on her tastebuds. She felt her face twisting with disdain, shuddering at the recollection of the lizard incident. 'I have had the misfortune to be in his presence only a few times over the years, his eyes are mean, he is of a vicious tongue. I have asked Mamma *why, why, why?* but Mamma is of the old world where one does not question the decisions of the man. My heart is tortured, for I love you so much, Alif, I cannot, do not, want to marry Malik, but I fear as a woman I have no say in the matter! It is tearing me apart; my heart is in shreds! Pappa has been talking about it again and again, excitedly, planning the wedding day. It makes me feel physically ill just listening to him. He asks of me, *Why are you so dismal and detached about your own wedding day, my little Yassie?* for I refuse to connect with him in conversation about it. I cannot tell him of my absolute wretched disdain for the marriage! I cannot tell him just the thought of being anywhere in the vicinity of that abhorrent Malik makes me want to be ill, for it is not a woman's place to have an opinion, particularly if it is different, it is considered disrespectful, disgraceful even.' Her words expelled rapidly, her shrilly tone escalating with her utter despair and frustration. She could feel the tears leaking from her soul once again.

Pausing for breath, she stopped, silent. The weight of the complexity of their situation hung heavily in the air between them. Her voice now low, she said, 'Malik always portrays to Pappa a man of standing, a man of goodwill, of integrity. He says everything that Pappa wants to hear from a future husband, a husband who is going to look after Pappa's only daughter—his words are very convincing. Pappa doesn't see the real Malik, as I do.' A deep sigh left her lips, a miserable sense of hopelessness seeping from her, as if time was running out. 'My time with you, my darling Alif, has opened the possibility of another world for me, a glimpse of something more in life, something I may be worthy of, something I can contribute to.' She gathered the edge of her skirt, lifting it to dab at her eyes. 'Do I dare hope for more, Alif?' Her voice was barely a squeak, so scared was she of what Alif's answer may hold.

CHAPTER 5

Alif - Then

Alif listened with intent as Yasmina divulged her news. Her voice came at him, brittle and raw with emotion. The brightness of their day had dulled, the energy suctioned out as if a vacuum had hoovered through the airspace of the barn, leaving only a despondency. He looked at the gold chain sparkling around his beloved's throat, glistening, exquisite against the purity of her skin, its beauty a stark contrast to the ugliness of their new reality. His heart ached hearing the wretched anguish discernibly etched in the utterance of her every syllable, each tumbling over the other, painfully escaping her lips, her nerves evidently fraught with heightened anxiety as she twisted and wrung her hands together. He could see her breaking, her goodness shattering into tiny shards of glass, the myriad pieces splintering through them both. The conniption of her words was not lost on him.

He was speechless. He had not been expecting such news. Perhaps they had been irresponsible, he thought to himself, having buried their heads in the sand like two ostriches, oblivious to reality, so enraptured in their own world. The enormity of her words sat heavily as they digested the reality of their situation. Silence.

Grasping at his jumbled thoughts, he tried to process the enormity of her words. The mere thought of losing her was incomprehensible. Of course, he acknowledged, he was firmly aware of the traditions and oppression of women in this country, his own country. It was an outdated system, the old patriarchal ways still prevalent throughout this part of the world, archaic, ideals that didn't serve a purpose or place in their changing society. Words of bitterness were stuck on the tip of his tongue. *But why am I confused?* he mused. *I am fully aware of the existence and the fundamentals of the patriarchal system of my country. Did I think I was immune to tradition, a system that had been in place for centuries?* Annoyance at his irresponsibility speared through his jagged thoughts.

Punishingly, an inner voice berated his selfish lack of foresight, his being blindsided by his own thoughtless emotions. He had been so enraptured with his love for Yasmina that he hadn't even paused to consider the situation he was potentially putting her in or considered any facts or logistics of their relationship moving forward, his judgment clouded with the here and now. His exasperation felt interminably thick, fuelled with frustration, his thoughts erratic, trying to puzzle together a solution to disentangle the two of them from the situation with which they were now confronted. He ploughed his hands through his hair, his fingers meeting with resistance, sticky from the hair gel he'd applied that morning. He twisted his body sideways, swiping his hands up and down the bale of hay behind him, wiping his sticky fingers, the sharpness of the hay akin to pinpricks, the result minimal. Clenching his fists, a heated frustration boiled through his veins. He inhaled long and deep, forcing the air into the depths of his lungs, holding his breath, the motion stabilizing him as he turned to Yasmina, trying to force a smile he was not feeling.

'Habiba.' He heard his raspy voice, weighted with emotion as he leaned gently toward her, enveloping her delicate hands within his own, his grip dulling the tremor quaking through her palms. Smiling lopsidedly, Yasmina peered at him through her long fringe. 'Maybe we can elope, Alif. Sail away. You, captain of our ship,' she said, her laugh a faint-hearted attempt to inject some lightness to balance the heaviness that now sat between them.

'If only, me lady,' Alif said, playing along with her. He ploughed on with his English impersonation, which had always brought a giggle out of her. 'We'd sail into the sunset and be mercenaries of the sea.' But his attempt also fell flat, a disparaged sigh of 'if only,' crawling from his lips. Yasmina disentangled her hands from his, a forced smile crinkling at the corners of her mouth, its strained rigour not reaching her eyes. The hint of their sailing away together was a fanciful dream, momentarily blanketing their reality. But neither of them was in the mindset for fanciful talk, the heartbreak of their reality sitting between them like the great white elephant in the room that it was. 'It's so unfair,' she pouted, rubbing her knuckles vigorously across her eye sockets, her small voice sounding childlike and miserable, laced with petulance, indicative of her youth. He tugged her hands away from her eyes, his rattled laugh laced with a pensive dose of despondency, 'You look like a red-eyed panda,' he joked, trying to buoy them both along on some semblance of lightness.

He clasped her delicate hands within his own, looking at her, his voice thick like molasses, 'Yasmina, I am so incredibly sorry.' His words sounded hollow, inadequate even to his own ears. 'Your pain pierces my heart.' Yasmina looked longingly at him, maybe wishing for something more tangible, a resolution, but they both knew that nothing he could say would erase the situation. Words were ineffective. He gently clasped her delicate face, turning it toward him, her beauty catching in his throat all over again, her obvious distress like a dagger plunging into the depths of his heart repeatedly. 'I am embarrassed to be of the male gender that has perpetrated this shameful history,' he whispered to her.

Alif knew his words of apology were empty, empty of resolution, and Yasmina's blank stare confirmed this, as she unfurled her hands from the bondage of her skirt, flattening it out, the creases deep, indicative of the depth of despair they were both feeling. *Sorry isn't going to change anything, rectify our situation, or help us.* 'Have you expressed your concerns to your Pappa, Yasmina?', he asked.

She tapped her foot on the floor nervously. 'No.' Her eyes were cast down. 'I dare not, Alif. The repercussions in the community of Pappa having a daughter who dared go against his wishes would be frowned upon.' Her voice was small. Alif knew how much she loved her Pappa. 'I could not do that to Pappa,' her voice interjected, hollowed out with sadness. 'So, now you understand my despair, Alif. I do not know what to do.' Her helplessness was unmistakeable. Restricted by invisible societal binds, expectations to comply, the unfairness of it all was frustrating. She looked so fragile sitting before him, he thought.

Leaning across, Alif took Yasmina's hands into his, unclenching her furled fingers, her nails leaving marks of scalloped indentations along her palms. The complexity of their situation hung in the air between them like an uninvited guest, their minds each trying to discern their unique set of circumstances.

Traffic of a Lie

Alif moved to rise, groaning, his body suddenly feeling older than his twenty-six years should. He turned, grasping Yasmina's hands, pulling her upright, holding her slender frame tight against his body. She moulded into him like a glove, the two of them fitting together like two pieces of the one puzzle they had become.

A rat sauntered past them, its oversized stomach grazing the floor. It was too obese to run, and it lazily ambled its path across the uneven dirt floor. It stopped midway, looking up at them, as if vexed at their presence, as though they were interrupting its freight route. Alif let out a startled screech, disgusted at the sight of the verminous creature, phobic to rodents. Yasmina, the country girl, was unperturbed by its presence. 'Not a fan of rats?' she jested, tickling him in the ribs, the sudden lighthearted atmosphere between them an enjoyable reprive, but short lived. The rat, apparently deciding to disregard them, continued its journey, labouring across the floor, out of sight, squeezing through the splintered wooden wall plank with its own mission to accomplish. 'If only we could disappear as easily as that rat just did,' Yasmina said with a sigh, her smile waning. She reached up, wrapping her arms around Alif's neck, her lips just inches from his. 'Why does life have to be so complicated?' It was a rhetorical question. The fanning of her breath against Alif's cheek felt sweet to him. 'What are we going to do, Alif?' Her face crumpled once again like a used tissue, the lightness of the moment dissipating.

Suddenly, as if a light switch had been flicked, a thought forms in Alif's mind, it's hazy outline slowly taking definition. He paused, swishing the thought around in his head, tasting the effectiveness of it, the realisation of what he must do becoming clear in his mind. A sliver of excitement built from within. Maybe their situation didn't have to be based on complications, he pondered. Squaring his shoulders, Alif disentangled Yasmina from their embrace, holding her at arm's length, needing to look her directly in the eye. He heard the conviction in his voice, riding out valiantly, his need primal in wanting to save them, to be her knight in shining armour. 'Yasmina, I shall speak with your father, I shall reason with him, I will ask for his blessing, that we be wed. I promise you; we shall be united because I love you, my darling, sweet Habiba. We belong together. I love you with all my heart, and nothing will keep us apart,' he spurted forth, his words escaping fast and furiously from his loose lips, flapping about, before his brain had time to assemble them into an intelligible concept.

Alif pulled Yasmina tight against his chest, wanting to protect her, cocoon her with his love. He felt her body deflate against him as if a balloon had burst in her lungs. She slowly expelled her breath, the expulsion long and airy, so deep into her depths had the balloon distended. She looked up at him, her mouth twisted to one side, a quirky trait she had when thinking. Alif watched with intent as the synapses of her brain slowly interpreted his words. The bleariness from the stains of her tears earlier were now being replaced with a smile, slowly spreading across her features, lighting up her eyes, lighting up her face. 'Alif', Yasmina's voice wobbled, barely audible, it was all she could muster, as she clasped his hands between hers, 'Alif, do you really think that is possible, that you really could talk to Pappa?'

CHAPTER 6

Alif – Then

Sighing deeply, Alif lifted his heavy head up from his cupped hands. The serenity of the scene before him had always had a calming effect in times past whenever troubled thoughts had clouded his mind. He admired the perfect symmetrical planting of the box hedges—hybrids specifically bred to withstand the heat of the climate in which they found themselves, along with the tall, graceful date palms often referred to as the tree of life, ramrod straight like sentries standing guard, articulated around the magnificent water feature. The ornately carved arbour was situated at the northern end of the pool, whitewashed and pristine, with its voile fabric adorning the structure, gently floating on the afternoon's scented breeze. Another deep sigh ballooned up from the depths of his soul; he felt the turbulence escaping through his pursed lips, the sight before him incongruous with the choppiness of the emotions tightly bound within him.

He nudged at a slightly elevated piece of bright yellow tile, gently lifting it with the toe of his shoe from the mosaic pattern laid out on the path before him. Feeling the pull of a smile creeping along the edges of his mouth slowly evolving into a grin, he felt a happy memory stir within his mind. One of him and Omar, his elder brother, the two of them helping Mohammed, one of the household handymen, piecing together the tiles, the colours bright, happy, two little boys studiously working side by side, amicably together, laughing with each other. Mohammed had been very accommodating, his guiding words gentle as he explained with patience to the two of them how to firstly map out the pattern they wished to lay, before gluing each piece individually into its appropriate place. Alif recalled the palm tree he had designed, his favourite tree, keeping with the ambience of the garden surrounded by multitudes of the trees. Omar, more ostentatious with his design, chose a bright yellow Lamborghini. The Lamborghini wasn't conducive with the aesthetics of the garden, and Mohammed had tried to dissuade him, but Omar had been insistent. 'Just like Uncle Abdul's,' he'd exclaimed with enthusiasm. 'I'm going to have my own Rambo Lambo one day, and soon!' Did you know that the Aventador design was inspired by an insect? How cool is that?' Omar's face had been lit up with exhilaration, he had always been a car buff. 'And also, the Italian police use Lamborghinis,' he'd boasted, suitably impressed. Mohammed had laughed and so, in accordance, had Alif. Omar's animated gesticulations had been infectious. And so, the Lamborghini had stayed.

Another time, another place, Alif thought, sighing, his mind returning to the present. He bent down to pick up the yellow tile, once bright, but now faded with time, dislodged from the front right fender of the Lamborghini. *I will ensure it is glued back into place*, he thought. Twirling the tile between his thumb and index finger, he reflected that the memory was of a time when life was simple, a time when life was easy and innocent, a time when their dearly beloved *walida* was still here on earth with them all. If he closed his eyes and concentrated hard enough, he could only just, all these years later, conjure up the essence of the woman he had loved more than life itself, his Mamma. The gentle touch of her embrace, her soothing, dulcet voice as she sang lullabies into his ear, the feeling of her hand as she stroked his hair. His dear, beautiful, beloved Mamma, a voice of wisdom, of explanation, always so understanding and nurturing of his gentle nature.

Her death had been sudden, most unexpected. He vividly remembered their father marching into their bedroom early one morning. He and Omar, aged ten and twelve respectively, were groggy from having been pulled from the depths of their sleep, and they struggled to comprehend the entirety of their father's words as he explained the new reality that they all now faced, the reality that Mamma had passed away during the night hours from a brain aneurysm. The two boys had had no idea what a brain aneurysm even was. Father had held himself rigid, and the pain had been evident in his vacant stare; his nerves were obviously frazzled. They found out later that he had been up all night at the hospital, pacing the 'family room' he and their closest family members had been allocated to, each of them there supporting Pappa at this, his most distressing time. The medical team, the best in the country, had done everything they possibly could to save Mamma's life, but the great bulging blood vessel in her brain, which burst voluminously, was beyond recovery; there was no possible chance of survival. Pappa had had to make the decision to turn off her life support.

Pappa's eyes had been dulled with sadness as he had sat on the end of Alif's bed. Alif had crawled out of the cocooned warmth of his doona onto Pappa's lap, Omar joining him on his brother's bed, both of them struggling to comprehend the news that their beloved Mamma was gone, a fact that would change their lives irrevocably. No one is ever truly prepared for the enormity of what the death of a loved one means, particularly as a child.

To have your security blanket pulled out from beneath you, to have the very person who gave you life, nurtured you, loved you unconditionally, suddenly be gone, without a goodbye, without warning, was an incomprehensible and devastating blow. Both the boys struggled to process the enormity of the words being conveyed to them, the words coming from Pappa's mouth. They had enjoyed afternoon tea with Mamma the previous day. They had sat there together, the three of them. How could that only be yesterday and yet today she was gone forever? Pappa had pulled Omar in closer, his big, strong arms enveloping them both into a clumsy hug. Alif's head had been nestled on Pappa's chest, his powerful and robust heartbeat thrumming in Alif's ears. Pappa's chin had rested on the top of both of their heads, his body shuddering, his contained sobs subdued as he wept quietly. He kept squeezing them both tightly, his actions jittery, simultaneously rubbing their arms up and down. Alif felt safe snuggled there, encapsulated in Pappa's strong arms, his familiarity, his scent, his strength all reassuring. The two boys had cried openly, noisily, as they tried to process the enormity of the news they had just been dealt. After a while, their sobs had subsided and the three of them had sat there, stone like, a numbness perpetrated by disbelief starting to wash over them. They hadn't wanted to move, safely ensconced in Pappa's arms, feeling as if their whole world had suddenly turned on its axis; it now felt destabilised.

Raya, their au pair, had appeared at their doorway, knocking quietly before entering, not waiting for a reply. Quietly she had directed her voice to Pappa, enquiring if he required assistance with the boys. Pappa had risen to leave, citing business; his voice had been thick with emotion, he had kissed them each before slowly leaving the room. Raya had helped them both back to their respective beds, even though on a normal day they would be getting up and dressed at this hour of the morning, preparing for their scholarly lessons. The sun's spidery rays were beginning to creep through the gap at their curtain's edge, heralding the new day dawning, basking their room in a thin light. But that day was far from normal. That day was to be their first day for the rest of their lives without their Mamma. They had lain in bed for some hours, both absorbed in their own pain.

'Omar.' Alif's voice was feeble, choked from all his crying. 'Do you think Mamma knew yesterday that she wouldn't be here today, wouldn't be here with us anymore on Earth?' he'd asked as he'd lain cocooned in his doona, in which he'd wrapped himself tightly. 'Where do you think she is now? Where does a person go when their heart stops beating? Do you think she felt her blood stop pumping when her heart stopped?' His jumbled thoughts tumbled out his mouth, his mind in overdrive. As hard as he tried to make sense of the situation, he couldn't process where Mamma was at this very moment. 'How can she be here one minute and not the next?' None of it made sense to him; he couldn't process the enormity of Mamma being gone.

'Just shut the hell up, Alif, with all your dumb questions,' Omar's voice had bellowed at him across the short space between their beds. But Alif hadn't been able to stop. He had needed answers. He had clambered out of bed and ventured down the long passageway in the western wing of their lodgings, calling for Pappa. 'Pappa, Pappa!' his voice bellowed, hysterics taking grip, the thought that perhaps they'd lost Pappa also magnifying in his mind. 'Pappa!' His last call had been long and drawn out as he ran, looking into every room as he passed.

'Hush, hush, Alif.' Raya appeared from the toy room, hurriedly. 'Why are you out of bed? You should be resting.' She had wrapped her arms around him comfortingly, stroking his head, the touch of her hand soothing.

'Raya.' He had been breathless. 'I need to know where Mamma is, please. I must know.' Desperation had rained out in Alif's voice, great big tears pooling in his eyes, overflowing like a waterfall, dripping onto his cheeks.

Taking his hand gently, leading him into the toy room, Raya had sat down on the large rocking chair located near the open window. The trickling sounds of the water softly cascading over the fountain outside seeped into the room, soothingly rolling in on the waves of the breeze. She drew him down onto her lap, cradling his head onto her bosom, slowly rocking back and forth.

The motion had been soothing and consoled his fragile state. 'My dear, sweet Alif,' she murmured into his ear. 'Hush, gentle child. Hush, hush.' Rocking him, she continued, 'Your Mamma will soon be joining the angels.' Sitting upright, he looked into her blue eyes, bewildered. 'But Raya, how how will Mamma do that? She does not have wings.' Confusion muddled his mind, and he was unable to comprehend Raya's words.

'Alif, when a person dies, their soul, not their earthly body, is taken by the Angel of Death,' Raya explained. 'And this Angel of Death is named Azra'il.'

'Is the Angel of Death a nice angel or a nasty angel?' he'd asked, screwing his face into a twisted look, trying to wrap his mind around this new concept. Raya paused; contemplation written across her face. She had looked at him earnestly, 'Azra'il helps God by transporting the souls of the deceased.' She paused, then said, 'so I suppose anyone who is being helpful is of a good nature.' She smiled at him then, but, staring back, Alif thought her smile looked crooked. Maybe Raya wasn't really sure, he surmised, and decided to not ask any more questions about Azra'il.

Raya had continued, her voice soft, 'God then sends two angels to question the waiting soul. If the questions are answered correctly, the good soul then sleeps during the Barzakh.'

He had interrupted again here and blurted out, 'But what happens if the questions are not answered properly, Raya? What happens then? What if Mamma didn't hear the question right, or didn't know how to answer?' His voice had risen into a shriek; he was terrified of the thought of Mamma getting her question wrong.

'If not answered correctly Alif, the soul is tormented by angels. This is known as punishment of the grave,' Raya had answered, her tone soft and measured. He had pondered Raya's words, weighing up all his love and feelings for Mamma.

'Mamma would have answered correctly because she always knew the right things to say, didn't she, Raya?' He had looked up at her earnestly as he tried to organize his nebulous thoughts into a logical context.. 'Mamma would now be sleeping, waiting to go to heaven as it is now the Barzakh,' his wobbly voice quivered as he tried to digest all this new information.

'Yes, Alif, your Mamma was a good lady. She would have said the right answers.' Raya's gentle words were comforting, and her explanation alleviated some of his distress.

'Now, come, dear child, let's go check on Omar and get you both washed up and off to the dining room for some lunch,' Raya had said, taking his hand. Digesting Raya's words, feeling satisfied with her explanation at knowing Mamma would soon be joining the angels, Alif had slid off her lap, taking her hand into his as they walked together back to his and Omar's bedroom. 'Raya', he said, his voice strong with conviction, assured of his decision, 'I don't want to ever die. I'm going to stay here always and forever with Pappa and Omar.'

Several days later, the funeral, an elaborate affair, their mother's life in its entirety was summed up in two hours, with prayers and wailing. Omar and Alif's tears had flowed freely. The funeral had been a fanciful occasion, with family, friends, and dignitaries all paying their respects, the call of prayer that day dedicated to Mamma. They had sat at the front, dressed in their finery, in all white, Pappa at their side. Alif had sat there picturing Mamma above them, her long, white feathery wings flapping delicately as she hovered overhead. She was smiling, which made him feel happy that she was happy. Without thinking he had taken hold of his brother's hand; Alif had wanted to help comfort him. Omar had snatched it away, a bitter scowl on his face. He was angry with Mamma for leaving them. Alif had tried to explain to him that Mamma was now an angel, but Omar said he was stupid for believing such a story, that angels weren't real.

But Alif knew otherwise, as he had seen Mamma; she had visited him the previous night as he'd dreamed. Mamma's sweet voice had whispered in his ear, telling him that everything would be all right, to have faith and that they needed to comfort and support each other. Alif really, really missed Mamma and wanted more than anything to have her here with them rather than with the angels, but Raya said it was best to accept that she wasn't ever coming back. Raya had explained that, once you crossed over with the angels, you stayed with God in His garden and if Alif behaved himself and was a good person, he would one day also go to God's Garden to be with Mamma. He decided then that he did want to die one day, so he could be with Mamma again and enjoy her garden with her—but not for a very long time as he still needed to learn lots more as he didn't have all the answers for the angels yet and he didn't want to get the questions wrong. He had tried very hard to explain all this to Omar, but he was way too angry to listen.

A week later, Pappa had entered their playroom, stopping just inside the doorway, dressed in his thobe, the long white garment pristine, his brown leather sandals silent on the tiled floor. Omar and Alif were sat solemnly, quietly, not play-fighting or interacting as they would normally be doing, each of them sipping their mint tea slowly, the *ghoriba bahla* cookies, always their favourites, normally devoured within seconds, untouched on the table before them. Zara the housekeeper had especially baked them earlier in an effort to try and cheer them up. They had both felt lethargic, a blanket of sadness weighing them down heavily since Mamma's funeral. Even though Alif knew that Mamma was an angel, it still hadn't stopped the grief from wrapping its sorrow into his body.

'Boys,' Pappa had begun, pausing wearily, speaking slowly. 'I understand how sad you both are, but we cannot undo what has been done. Mamma is not coming back.' He emphasised the word *not*. 'Life is unfair at times. Situations arise and happen that we cannot control, but when these occurrences do arise, we must dig deep into our souls to find the strength to be able to move forward through the emotions and the pain.' *Mamma's death was an occurrence.* The erratic thought flittered through Alif's mind. He banked it in his 'questions to ask Raya' part of his mind, needing to know exactly what Pappa meant. His attention drew back to Pappa's voice as he continued; his message was direct, delivered without deliberation: 'You are not babies anymore; a few more years and you will be men. As such, it is time to man up, to demonstrate courage and fortitude, for the situation cannot be reversed. It is alright to mourn, but you must do so in private.'

They had both looked up at Pappa, who'd delivered his words without empathy.

'Easier said than done, Pappa,' Omar had scowled under his breath; Pappa hadn't heard, for he had already turned on his heel, departing. From that day onward, Alif had never cried in the vicinity of others another tear for his beloved mother, the angel. The expectation at ten years of age was to 'be a man, strong, stoic . . . never let another see your weakness,' but his tears had rolled uncontrollably and unashamedly down his cheeks every night for months, each droplet of sorrow leaking from his soul, absorbed in the luxurious duck down feather pillow along with his gut-wrenching sobs. He had wanted his Mamma, the angel, back.

And now, years later, he felt his tears coursing down his cheeks again. His tears were raw, unaltered anguish, flowing for another woman that he loved with all his heart, knowing that tradition dictated that it was a love he could not pursue. Without thinking he had declared to his beautiful Yasmina that he would talk to her Pappa. He would reason with him, explain their situation, convince her father of their love; his expectation was that her Pappa would accept their decision unequivocally, without resistance, without question. His statement had filled Yasmina with hope, a hope now upon reflection he realised was false. Having hope without substance was more crushing than facing the reality. How thoughtless he had been in his rushed promises, his heart ruling his head, his words blurted out foolishly before thinking through the implications, the realities, or the repercussions. How could he approach Yasmina's father, ask for her hand in marriage, promise a life for her, one that was completely foreign to their own? To do so would undermine Khalif, bring shame upon him, upon his integrity, his honour, an unwritten line that is never crossed.

He recalled Yasmina's summations, her anguish at finding out that she was to be betrothed to Malik, a consanguineous marriage, a normality in regional areas of their country, an honour to the bride's family. She had described the process of Malik and his family's first visit, bearing gifts, asking her father for her hand in marriage. Yasmina had explained how she had shrivelled inside, feeling like a lamb being led to the slaughter, a sacrifice. But her father Khalif had burst with pride for the daughter he had raised, a young woman capable of fulfilling the ultimate role of wife and mother, tentative to serving her husband, bearing him children, tending their home. He had instilled in her obedience and subservience—admirable qualities a husband looks for in a wife.

And Alif, you absolute fool, he thought, admonishing himself, you have misled Yasmina in the belief that they could be together, that you could talk her father around to the idea of them being wedded, knowing the truth in his heart that the reality wasn't possible. Yasmina was betrothed to another man, a decision that could not be undone.

CHAPTER 7

Yasmina – Then

The big day had arrived. The house was bustling with excitement, bursting at its seams. Yasmina closed her bedroom door, needing to shut out the buzzing of happiness that was flitting throughout the rest of the house, preferring the sombre mood of her own company. She sat staring at herself, not recognizing the image from the mirror staring back at her. She looked down at the heavy, dark blue brocade dress she was wearing, hating everything the dress signified. Its inky colour reflected her mood, mimicking the dark circles of despair under her eyes, evidence of her countless sleepless nights of the past weeks. Here it was. Her. Wedding. Day. The mere thought of 'the day' had made her physically ill, on several occasions she'd vomited, the bile spewing forth, an extension of the pessimism that had settled heavy, like a ton of bricks across her soul.

She knew she'd been difficult and unappreciative leading up to this day, childishly sabotaging wedding plan conversations, refusing to participate, but she hadn't been able to contain herself—such was the intensity of her feelings.

Pappa had been discombobulated by her behaviour, her clearly discernible petulance. Her lack of interest, appreciation, or consideration to participate in any wedding discussions had concerned him, driven him to frustration. Her voice had been snippety with every conversation with Pappa of late, her words impenitent, firing sharpened arrows, aimed directly at him. She knew her words had hurt Pappa; his look of wounded surprise reflected back at her through sorrowful eyes as he'd absorbed the brunt of her frequent outbursts. *But I am unapologetic*, she thought, her wounded heart unable to accommodate or consider Pappa's feelings at this point.

Putting it down to wedding day nerves, Pappa had been undeterred by her behaviour and, after giving Malik his blessing for her hand in marriage, he had set to immediately making plans. He was generally a man of few words, and his feverish excitement had been entirely out of character. Presumably the generous gifts of the dowry had fuelled Pappa's fervour. Yasmina had concluded this, for she couldn't fathom any other reason why he had given his blessing in the marriage.

Pappa had announced one night over the evening meal, his words tumbling excitedly over each other, he spoke so quickly, 'I have it! We shall renovate the ramshackle old back barn and revel in the best wedding festivities you've ever seen,' He'd thumped his fist noisily down on the old wooden table for affirmation. Yasmina had physically baulked at the announcement, nearly choking on the hot and sweet *zalook* she was nibbling at, the eggplant and peppers lodging in her throat, the very suggestion of Pappa's idea putrid and offensive. *Oh, the irony'*, she'd groaned, devastated at the thought that the wedding would take place in the barn where Alif and she had met. It was their special place, their place of hope and joy, and now it would be tarnished with the seeds of dread.

Karim's eyes had flitted sideways in her direction, widened like saucers, at Pappa's suggestion, the thought obviously passing his mind also, whilst simultaneously plastering a smile on his face, as he looked across the table at Pappa. 'We will put in a new floor to dance the night away on, a servery for the finest feast you've ever seen in these parts—tangines, lamb, harira, makouda, harissa and so much more.' Pappa's delight escalated, his voice flourishing on the waves of excitement. Standing, he had drawn Mamma up beside him, twirling her around on the spot. 'We will invite all near and far to celebrate our beautiful Yassie. She will be the talk of the district, her beauty, her accomplishment!'. Accomplishment! Yasmina had nearly choked, the infarction of her indignation lodging in her throat. She had felt faint. *She hadn't accomplished anything, she had been handed over to Malik like a prized possession, with no input whatsoever on her behalf,* the thought angry in her mind.

It was all too much and, feeling overwhelmed, she had excused herself from the table, needing to get away from this farcical nightmare that had become her life. She'd thrashed open the lean-to door, and it had banged heavily against the wall as she had stormed outside, the warm evening breeze greeting her. Setting off at a pace, she thudded through the dark paddocks, the howling of a golden jackal echoing in the distance, its mournful sound paralleling her mood. Unperturbed by the night sounds, she had scuttled along the narrow dirt track leading to the front paddock where the goats were stabled. The goats had stirred, sensing Yasmina's arrival; Bambi bleated as she frolicked over to greet her. Bambi's beautiful doe-shaped eyes had looked up at Yasmina inquisitively as if she'd picked up on her mistress's dampened mood. Yasmina had leaned on the fence, scratching the soft fur of Bambi's head. She had stood still as she watched the shadows of a few of the other goats as they slowly moved about, disturbed from their rest by her presence.

Her emotions had been wrought, hammered out of shape by the whole sorry mess that had become her life. Sulking, she stayed with the goats for quite some time, taking refuge in the comfort of their easiness, unburdening them with her thoughts. She was grateful for the dark solitude that had enveloped her like a black cloak, her mind a murky quagmire. A headache had started to ebb at her temples, the pain rendered from the countless thoughts rampaging through her brain, a warring battle of contemplation, frustration and enragement. 'What is the point?' she asked dejectedly, looking down at Bambi, her voice quivering, as Bambi rubbed her head fervently against Yasmina's hand. Feeling futile, Yasmina finally traipsed back to the house, where all was quiet with the sounds of the sleeping.

A discreet knock at her bedroom door brought her back to the now. Mamma entered, quietly clicking the door closed behind her. 'You OK, Yassie?' Mamma's garlic breath permeated her nostrils as she leaned over and planted a gentle kiss on her cheek. She nuzzled into Mamma's ample bosom, a place of comfort and security. 'Yasmina, why can't you be happy . . . be grateful for what you can have?' Mamma's soft breath feathered across her cheek, her words pausing as if she'd chosen them wisely, 'and not yearn for something that's not yours to take? Is it so bad that you will have a husband who can provide for you, look after you, create a family with you?'

Sitting up, she stared at Mamma, gulping in the essence of her, her goodness. She was a quiet, unassuming lady who had always accepted her position in life, giving unconditionally to those around her, never thinking of herself or her needs, her mere existence selfless.

Mamma's words only furthered her sorrow. She wanted so much more from her own life than what Mamma had had. She yearned to be able to make her own decisions, her own choices, not to be somebody's appendage, somebody's chattel. She wanted to live and love freely, to travel, experience the world, love on her own choosing. She wanted to build a life with Alif. She wanted to share and experience all of this and so much more with her beloved Alif.

Gulping, she closed her eyes, the emotions of her subconscious swirling like a tornado. She was overwhelmed with guilt, a feeling of selfishness filling her, selfishness for sabotaging Mamma and Pappa's plans for her. They had always loved her unconditionally, and now here she was throwing it all back in their faces with belligerence because she wanted to follow her own path. *Is it so wrong for me to feel this way?*

Inadequately, her voice small, Yasmina said, 'Mamma, if I could be half the woman you are, I would feel blessed, honoured . . . but I'm not like you.' These last words a mere whisper from her lips. A quietness settled between them, each deep in contemplation, the sands shifting beneath their worlds, before Mamma, drawing in her breath deep, slowly murmured, 'Child, you must do what is right and not what is lust.' Her words were quiet and measured, and she paused, as if to allow them to sink in. Yasmina was stung by Mamma's words and rolled the warning around in her mouth. Its taste was vulgar and offensive, and she spat them out in rejection, her hackles rising instantly. She didn't appreciate the tone of Mamma's advice, as if she was denigrating what she and Alif had as some lustful infatuation. She hadn't told Mamma of Alif, and her love for him. As far as she was aware, Mamma didn't know of his existence, yet her words seemed to suggest otherwise, their tastelessness hanging in the air.

Yasmina sat up, bristling, but Mamma didn't seem to notice or else chose not to, continuing, 'For to not do so will only end in discontent and heartache.' Her tone suddenly brisk, a dismissive rejection of her feelings, as if sweeping them away, under the carpet, out of sight and out of mind. 'Now, hush, hush, my dear one.' Mamma's tone was soothing again, the switch confusing her, as she stroked her head, looping her fingers through her long, loose curls. 'Women like us don't have the luxury of choices; we have a duty to honour. Is it so bad to be a nurturer, a homemaker?' A bewilderment was attached to Mamma's voice, as if daring that Yasmina would contemplate anything else. 'I love you and Karim more than life itself,' Mamma continued, her tone so soft now she was barely audible, her face turned toward the window, a wistful look clouding her eyes as she gazed through the curtains. . . . 'Sometimes we must do what is expected, which isn't always the same as what we want for ourselves. Why can't you be happy, Yasmina, grateful? Malik comes from a reasonable family.' Her voice faltered as she stumbled over the word *reasonable*. 'He can provide for you, look after you. Life will be so much easier for you if you can just accept your destiny.'

Yasmina sat up, detaching herself from Mamma's embrace, offended by her words, but not surprised. She bit her tongue, holding in the exasperated words of annoyance that were lodged there, as it was evident that words and discussions were pointless at this stage. Their reasonings poles apart. Mamma slowly stood up, staring at Yasmina, sighing as if she had also reached the same realization. 'Compose yourself, prepare for the festivities of the day ahead,' she murmured, before quietly leaving her bedroom, firmly clicking the door behind her.

Yasmina sat, looking unseeingly at the back of her bedroom door, her fluffy brown dressing gown hanging from its hook, limp without her in it. Mamma's parting words weighed down with a conflicting heaviness on her heart. She deliberately hadn't told Mamma about Alif, for that was her sacred secret and hers alone, but from Mamma's words she had the feeling she'd guessed—mothers' intuition, perhaps? Yasmina sat for a while, pondering her words, her hands once again twisting and kneading the voluminous fabric of her dress into knots, the bulky material crumpled and folded, creating little spiralling peaks across her lap. She had always known what the expectation of her role in life would be, but maybe, just maybe she had dared to hope for something more. *Foolish is as foolish does* barked through her thoughts, an annoying saying of Aunt Sabrina's, as she heard her aunt's voice echoing through the hallway. Alif had opened her mind to other possibilities. *Am I a fool to consider these possibilities?* she considered. The dark cloud of questions swirled around again, taking hold in her mind like a low-pressure weather system ready to burst. Despair enveloped her once again.

Forcing herself upright, Yasmina let her gown drop, not bothering or caring to straighten the twisted crinkles of knotted fabric. She could hear Aunt Sabrina's voice calling her, before a loud rapping of knuckles vibrated through her door, followed by the splintering shrill of her piercing voice. 'Yasmina, come, come!' Unable to help herself, issuing orders as always. Yasmina groaned, her newly acquired constant grumble of dread dripping from her lips. Reluctantly, she hauled herself from the comfort of her bedroom, the rapping splintering through the doorway again with ferocity, the thin door vibrating on its hinges. She threw her Aunt Sabrina an acknowledgment of a response, that she was nearly ready. A loose thread hanging from her dress caught on the jagged edge of her middle fingernail, hooking the gold thread, unravelling it the length of her dress. Unperturbed, she let it hang, a loose thread the least of her problems. Opening her door, the commotion of the house assaulted her, the ruckus more aligned with a circus than a wedding, she thought, ironically.

As she stepped into the hallway one of Karim's kittens darted through her feet, taking her off guard, its little eyes manic, her two-year-old cousin Lillyanna in close pursuit, her little lungs bellowing almighty squeals of glee and delight, flapping her chubby arms about as she tried to catch the poor, frightened kitten. 'Lilly, Lilly.' Yasmina bent over to distract the little girl, trying to wrap her up in her arms. But Lilly had other ideas and kicked and squealed, being held obviously not on her agenda. Before Yasmina realised it, the kitten had darted out from under the hidey-hole the volumes of her skirt had provided, its little claws hooking into the hem of her skirt. Frantically trying to free itself, the kitten thrashed about, gold embroidery threads unravelling from the tearing of threads. Yasmina was now holding Lilly, who was kicking and thrashing about in glee at sighting the kitten again.

Aunt Sabrina appeared, clapping her hands, admonishing Yasmina for her childish behaviour, taking Lilly out of her arms and simultaneously unhooking the trapped kitten before kicking it down the hallway. 'For the love of Allah, Yasmina, look at you,' she tutted, her eyes roaming the state of her dress. Ignoring her, Yasmina pushed past, walking through into the kitchen, her frazzled nerves twisted with dread with the knowledge that she must go through with this farce of a marriage.

Their small kitchen was bursting with excitement. Family from near and far had congregated at their little home. Aunt Sabrina's shrill voice could be heard above the hustle and bustle. The bloody woman was everywhere, the self-delegated captain, Yasmina thought miserably. Sabrina's sharp voice rose again, issuing orders. 'Karim and Khalid!' Her shrill voice was not unlike a banshee monkey, Yasmina thought, annoyed, as it pierced through their kitchen doorway. 'Take these dishes now, boys. Put them on the wagon to be taken to the barn, with haste.' She clapped her hands together as if to confirm the urgency, her bulky figure dominating a large space in their tiny kitchen. Yasmina watched the boys manoeuvring carefully around Aunt Sabrina, obediently gathering a dish in each hand, walking slowly to keep the dishes balanced, the aromas intoxicating. They felt important to be bestowed with such a task, the concentration etched on their faces intense.

Yasmina looked about herself, her eyes devouring the work of grandeur Mamma had orchestrated—*all for me*, she sighed. Such a lavish event as a wedding celebration called for an absolute feast and Mamma, with the help and input of her sisters, hadn't disappointed. The delicious aromas of lamb, chicken and camel dishes left the kitchen one by one, carefully being delivered to the barn. Yasmina quietly eased over to her beautiful Jadda, who had been relegated by Aunt Sabrina to the corner by the stove, out of the way—Yasmina's dear, sweet granny who lived with Aunty Layla, her mother's sister.

'Hello, Jadda,' Yasmina whispered, folding her grandmother's weathered hands into hers, squeezing them gently before planting a kiss on either cheek, hugging her, devouring the sense of calm and security her darling granny exuded. She gently retrieved her right hand from Yasmina's, touching it to her heart. 'My beautiful, beautiful Yassie. I feel the bleakness in your heart.' Yasmina gasped, surprised by Grannie's insight, her accuracy alarming. She cast her eyes downward, wishing to deflect the conversation from herself, scared of Grannie's compassion opening the floodgates of her tears again, feeling that it was pointless at this stage to discuss her feelings anyway—no one had listened this far.

'How are you in all this commotion, Granny?' Yasmina's voice was barely audible as she flipped the dialogue. Granny seemed to take the cue as she looked at her, her face inches from her own. 'I am grand, dear child. Just grand.' Her raspy voice was a whisper. 'Such a celebration. Your Pappa is so proud of you.' She spread her arm out and flowed it across the bustle in front of them. Frowning, a deep line creating a canyon between her eyes, her wrinkled face depicting a lifetime of hard work on the land, she said, 'But why are you wearing blue, Yasmina?'

She looked down at her dress, at the dark inky blue of it, the memory of the argument that had erupted between Pappa and her over her choice of wedding regalia fresh in her mind. Yasmina had been petulant, her childish behaviour rearing its ugly head again, a behaviour generally uncharacteristic of her personality, but common of late—a behaviour of which she wasn't proud. Disregarding the tradition of wearing green and gold, she had defiantly chosen the blue dress, just to be difficult, to assert her independence, which had been much to Pappa's disappointment. Yasmina wasn't proud of herself. 'Why are you so determined to sabotage your own wedding?' Pappa had implored despairingly, wringing his hands together, a spasm of pain crossing his normally tranquil features. 'Why can't you just be happy, Yassie?' He had stood there solemnly before turning and walking out of the room.

Yasmina tried to hide the tears brimming in her eyes, evoked at the memory, the look of disappointment on Pappa's face. She didn't even recognise herself anymore. Since the betrothal, a black haze had taken over her mind and soul, a darkness she couldn't control, couldn't shake off. *This should be the happiest time of my life, but it felt like the worst.* She tried to discreetly wipe away her tears, patting her eyes with her sleeve, but her tears did not go unnoticed by Grannie's shrewd eyes of perception. 'To dream of something more than what is our destiny in life, Yasmina, is to delegate yourself to a life of sadness and misery, a life of what ifs? We must be grateful for what we have as opposed to yearning for what we cannot have.' The older woman's voice of wisdom, her words of advice, were incredulous as Yasmina's ears absorbed it. 'Oh, Granny, if only you knew,' she whispered, leaning across into her ear. 'If only you knew.'

'It is time.' Sabrina's shrilly screech interrupted them. 'To the barn, everyone.' Clap, clap, turning her head, she hissed at the vacant airspace next to her to 'shut up.' Yasmina looked at her aunt, bewildered. She acted like a madwoman at times, she thought. Turning to Granny, she helped raise her to her feet, her arthritic body creaking with the exertion, before kissing her again on each cheek. Granny reciprocated, her rheumy eyes looking right inside her, and squeezed her hands. 'Allow yourself to be happy, dear child, and the black clouds will lift.' A gasp escaped Yasmina's lips, as she was taken aback again by Grannie's accuracy of being able to read her feelings, her insight. She stepped back to allow her to pass as everyone left the kitchen and Pappa arrived.

CHAPTER 8
Khalif - Then

Khalif walked across the dry, parched ground toward the goats' corral. He could hear voices of glee and clapping floating across the airwaves, the sounds being carried by the slight breeze as he approached his daughter. Reaching Yasmina, he rested his arm in a gentle embrace of affection across her shoulders. *My beautiful Yassie, as they all so affectionately called her*, he thought, the abbreviation of her name coming into effect when Karim as a toddler couldn't pronounce Yasmina. Yasmina is leaned against the rickety fence line, her arms folded in front of her, leaning on the top barrier creating a curvature to allow her protruding abdomen to tuck in under her. Her waiflike figure at odds with her heavily extended belly, the baby due soon. He was filled with love as he looked at his daughter—for her and for the impending arrival of his granddaughter. Thinking back, his mind retrieved a happy memory when they had first found out about Yasmina's pregnancy. *Had that only been a few months ago? So much had changed in such a short time frame,* he reflected. Fatima had been adamant right from the beginning that the baby was a girl. After much persuasion, counteracted with equal objections from Yasmina, Fatima had finally convinced her daughter to allow her to do the gender prediction test. Yasmina had eventually complied with her mother's wishes and had lain on her back as directed. Fatima had proceeded to drop an insect on their daughter's expanding abdomen, the insect landing on its back. 'It's a girl, it's a girl!' Fatima had clapped with glee, her eyes glistening, moist. She had reached out, grabbing Yasmina and pulling her into an upright position. Filled with delight, Fatima had wrapped her arms tightly around their daughter, such had been her happiness. 'The bug test was accurate with both you and Karim and all of Layla's children,' Fatima had declared excitedly, her voice singsong as she referenced Layla, her sister, their neighbour some five miles away who had seven children.

'Then it must be correct, my darling Fatima,' he had said, caught up in her excitement, laughing with her, the two of them embracing Yasmina together.

Without ado, Fatima had set about knitting and weaving—blankets, shawls, wraps, booties, and jumpers, every item in pink, her fingers flying across the needles or loom. The sound of the knitting needles had rhythmically clicked between Fatima and him every evening as they'd enjoyed a cup of tea before bed. The memory momentarily sang in Khalif's heart, making him happy, before his thoughts were snapped, like an overstretched elastic band, back to the present, the sound, a loud sigh emitted by Yasmina. To his shock, he visibly felt her shudder, her body quivering under his touch, an uneasiness transcending into her eyes . . . *as if he repulsed her*?

Taken aback, his heart lurched with pain. *How did we come to this*? he thought sadly. *He had always shared a close and special bond with Yasmina.* Deciding to ignore her shudder, he leaned in close. 'How are you, Yassie?' At that moment a Chiffchaff lands on the wooden railing nearby, it's warbling buoyant, unpretentious, incognizant to the heaviness hanging in the air around it. Khalif glances at the bird, waiting for Yasmina to respond.

Yasmina slowly turned toward her father, acknowledging his presence, her forlorn eyes looking up. 'OK, Pappa.' Her monotone response was unconvincing, her body language despondent, suggesting otherwise, a saddening sigh escaping her lips.

'Good show.' Khalif bowed his head right, gesturing toward the corral. 'You taught Karim well.'

'Yes.' Her response was monosyllabic.

The silence stretched before them, the air pulsing with tension of words unsaid. An air of resignation seemed to emanate from his daughter.

'You want to talk?'

He threw the question into the abyss. Drawing in his breath, long and hard, he holds it, a balled knot of anticipation, lodged deep in his chest. A longing of hope clings to him, that his daughter may reciprocate, may bridge the canyon that has opened like a bottomless chasm between them. He notes a clouded expression cross Yasmina's features, as if she also is grappling internally with her own thoughts. Silence stretches once again between them, long and drawn out.

'Mischa, Baron, Rose, correct.' Karim's voice rose above the hubbub of the spectators' murmurs, breaking the shield of silence standing between father and daughter, the goats responding to their master's command.

Khalif sighed, directing his attention to the goats. Their surefootedness was admirable. Each nimbly and effortlessly navigated the branches of the majestic old tree, the cork oak, which was devoid of leaves. The tree was beautiful in its skeletal appearance, the gnarled bark, bumpy and thick, strong branches providing the perfect structure for the goats to bound along. His mind reflected back. . . . When Yasmina had been a young girl, randomly, this one day, she had been out in the goat corral when several of the goats had mounted the tree, bounding from branch to branch. Delighted, Yasmina had started teaching them to respond to commands. Some months later a tour bus had been passing by, detoured from its usual route at the request of a passenger wanting to glimpse an 'authentic' look at the 'real' farmlands rather than just the premium tourist stops. It had been a wonderful surprise to the tour director when he sighted this slip of a girl commanding her herd of goats. He had stopped the bus immediately, enabling his passengers to enjoy the spectacle before them. The bus group had been delighted watching the agility and prowess of the goats as well as the young girl directing her herd. From this random encounter the 'goat shows' had evolved.

Khalif, naturally delighted at this opportunity to raise much-needed extra funds for the farm, had purposed a 'viewing arena' fashioned from old timber, the posts lashed together with binding rope. Word spread and the accolades were favourable. 'Unapologetically rustic, primitive and innocent,' 'authenticity of the backbone of the country,' 'a must-see, genuine in its presentation and no-pretentiousness.' The reviews in the national papers soon made headlines.

Karim's voice interjected, bringing Khalif's thoughts back to the present. 'Bambie, Rashad . . . mount'. Obeying gleefully, bounding up the branches effortlessly, the goats reacted excitedly to the sound of Karim's commands. The tourists clapped enthusiastically; their glee obvious, genuine enjoyment etched on their faces. Khalif had taken to being present at each showing, ensuring his children weren't exploited in any way.

'Good show, son.' He firmly patted Karim on the back. Karim's beaming smile lit up his face as he looked up to his father. 'Thanks, Pappa, the crowd really enjoyed themselves today,' he responded with obvious pride to the encouragement, puffing his chest out.

'I'd better get this lot back under control,' the young boy stated, laughing as his eyes roamed over his herd of goats, who were now cavorting about before him. 'Moosh, moosh,' He spread his arms wide and the goats, understanding their master's command, began to frolic obediently back into their paddock.

George the bus driver approached Khalif, extending his hand for a firm handshake. He handed Khalif the gratuities envelope, the money collected en route. George, an unlit cigarette hanging from his lips, causing his speech to slur, bent his head, lighting the cigarette. He inhaled deeply and turned his head to the side, blowing out a long cloud of smoke, a low guttural sound exhaling from the back of this throat. 'Your boy did well, you must be proud,' he said, his tobacco-stained teeth showing, nodding in Karim's direction. He had come to know Yasmina and Karim well over the past few years driving this route. 'Thank you, young man. We loved your show.' Cheers and whoops of praise reached across the yard, called out from the delighted tourists as they lined up to reboard the bus.

'Karim, well done!' George's gravelly voice called out across the corral, Karim raising his hand in acknowledgement.

'Thank you, George.' The young boy's voice was filled with exuberance before he disappeared inside the small barn. 'Yes, I am very proud, he's a good lad,' Khalif responded to George's statement. 'What's up with Yasmina? She looks sad every time I see her lately,' George asked, his eyes diverting to where Yasmina was still leaning crouched over the rail. 'She not happy in her marriage?'

George's astute observation took Khalif by surprise. Not knowing how to answer, Khalif left the question to pass, chewing it over in his mind. George, noting his passengers were all on board, stubbed his cigarette butt on the ground, grinding it into the dirt with his heel. 'Well, better get this lot to their next destination,' he stated succinctly. They shook hands again. 'See you next time, George.' He departed with a wave.

Walking back around to the east side of the corral to where Yasmina was standing, Khalif ventured again, 'How are you, Yasmina?' He rested his arm around his daughter's shoulder once again, studying her face. Her difficult behaviour during the lead-up to the wedding and subsequent ceremonies had been contradictory to her personality. He hadn't liked or understood this side of his daughter's personality and found her discontent perplexing. His Yasmina. She had always been of a gentle, caring and obedient nature, accepting of their life on the land, knowledgeable of her future's format. Therefore, it had been out of her character when she had suddenly become defiant and difficult during the wedding preparations, as if she was intent on sabotaging her own marriage. He had noticed prior, on occasions, her sneaking off to the back barn, the dreamy look on her face upon returning to the house, the distant look in her eyes, her disconnection from family discussions. He knew this could only mean one thing but hadn't discussed his concerns with Fatima. Best to leave sleeping dogs lying, he had thought. To voice his concerns would give concerns to a voice, initiating and allowing conversation that would serve no benefit. *We are people of the land, our lives simple and uncomplicated in the knowledge of our place on the societal ladder. To think anything other was foolish*, he thought. Yes, Yasmina had intelligence of mind, reading and absorbing whatever she could get her hands on. Fatima had encouraged this constant thirst for knowledge, this yearning to know more about the world around her. It had bothered him so. He had raised Yasmina to understand that a woman's place was to create a home, rear the children, serve her husband. He had tried to make her understand that they were rich in their own way, rich in their abundance of love. They had a roof over their heads, food on their table. He had tried to instil in her that to accept one's vocation in life was the key to happiness. It wasn't about getting all that you want in life, it was about accepting and enjoying all that you had. He had explained to his daughter that they had everything they needed, as she also would when she created her new life with her husband.

His mind wandered back to Yasmina and Malik's wedding day. Sabrina, shrewd in observation, had been contrite with him at the wedding: 'Yasmina's sanctimonious behaviour has not gone unnoticed.' Her voice had screeched above the music of the wedding celebrations, discretion having never been one of her attributes. Bossy by nature for as long as he could remember, Sabrina had never shied away from voicing her opinions.

'She should be grateful to have the opportunity of such a wonderful husband as Malik,' she'd continued, spitting out the words vehemently, indignant that anyone would think her son not worthy. 'She would do well to remember her place!' Khalif had been abhorred by his second cousin's inappropriate outburst, yet, surprised by his own admission of partially agreeing with her words.

Yasmina had been sanctimonious. 'Hush, Sabrina, Yasmina is grateful.' His eyebrows knitted together in anguish, and he carefully chose his words for he needed to calm the situation not fan the flame he could see firing in Sabrina's eyes. His words had been placating. 'With the generosity of heart and diligence to duty you have raised a very fine young man indeed.' Sabrina, liking what she was hearing, had smiled. 'And Yasmina is by far a lucky woman,' he had added. 'It's just the nerves . . . they've gotten the better of her.' His words tumbled over themselves in his haste to placate the bombastic woman standing before him. 'Yasmina will do you proud, mark my words,' he'd stated.

'For her sake, let's hope the apple doesn't fall far from the tree,' came Sabrina's ugly retort, which wasn't lost on him. Her caustic personality was her most unattractive trait.

Sighing, Khalif felt heavy. Weariness weighed him down. His mind continued to spiral backward; Sabrina filled his thoughts. She had always harboured a nasty attitude toward Fatima, vicious words glided easily off her tongue. Like a hot knife through butter, Sabrina's jealous streak had possessed a sharpness to it. This feud, dated back to her childhood, perpetuated by her own parents. Sabrina and Fatima had grown up on adjoining land holdings, however Fatima had born from a marginally wealthier family, with more connections, a better upbringing and Fatima herself prettier, more liked and respected than Sabrina had ever been. The feud generational, apparently linked to some land claimed by Fatima's family, supposedly belonging to Sabrina's family. There had never been any evidence to substantiate this feudal accusation. Like a volcano, bubbling and brewing under the surface, so to had Sabrina's jealousy. She had this fanciful idea that Fatima 'owed her', being the 'thief she was, taking their land.' It was of course a ludicrous accusation, but it hadn't stopped Sabrina's own insecurities being manifested against Fatima. It didn't help either that as a child Fatima was loved and respected by her parents, admired by the locals for her manners, her selfless acts of helping teach the younger children at prayer time and donating her time to help clean the local mosque. Sabrina's own dysfunctional upbringing devoid of love and kindness had only spurned her jealousy of Fatima. At times Khalif felt like he was caught in the middle of the two women. A peacemaker. Fatima, his wife, who had his complete devotion and support and then Sabrina, who was family and therefore someone he had to put up with, accommodate.

He had been surprised when Sabrina had approached him, asking for Yasmina's hand in marriage for her son Malik, a dowry on offering. Khalif had taken this as a peace offering. Malik had seemed like a decent young man on the few occasions Khalif had previously met him. He'd had no reason to doubt Malik's pledged commitment to Yasmina. Khalif had posed many questions to Malik, wanting to ensure that he was of genuine context, a man of integrity, worthy of his daughter's hand in marriage. Malik had assured him he would be a good husband to Yasmina, promised that he would care and provide for her as they build their lives together. He'd spoken logically and with conviction, sincerity had sounded in his words, leaving Khalif no cause for doubt.

Pausing, his thoughts dishevelled, Khalif rubbed his hand across the back of his head, the tension tight. He felt like one of those clowns at the circus, juggling myriad balls, trying not to drop one of them and upset the balance. The sounds of the present snapped his thoughts back to the now. Yasmina was still next to him.

'Good show,' he said again, his head bowing right, gesturing toward the corral. 'You taught Karim well.'

'Yes.' Her acknowledgment was again monosyllabic, a whisper. The silence, a new stranger to their relationship, stretched out before them, the air seeming to pulse with unsaid rigidity. 'You want to talk?' He threw the question into the ring for the second time, hoping Yasmina may reciprocate. Floundering, he was at a loss for how to reach out to his daughter, communication having never been his strong point. He was a man of action, not words. A long pause abrades the airspace between them, pulsating with tension. Eventually, barely audible, his daughter's voice little more than a whisper. 'No'. Her rejection was like a knife through his heart.

CHAPTER 9

Yasmina – Then

Pappa approached, putting his arm over her shoulders, quietly throwing out the question, 'you want to talk', the words landing in the void between them. Yasmina knew his embrace was a loving gesture, but involuntarily she shuddered at his touch. The grey fog that had gradually been spreading its tentacles through her brain was insidiously tightening its grip. It was one she welcomed, a fog of indifference, without feeling. Her malignant mood was slowly numbing her, a reprieve since her marriage, since Alif had let her down. She now knew that Alif's words of speaking with Pappa, of coming for her, were empty. The thought of Alif coming for her was now an abandoned dream. Her reality was with Malik, her nightmare. She struggled to accept this fact.

We were so in love, he promised me. What went so terribly wrong? Yasmina asked herself. *Did Alif decide that I wasn't enough? Did he realise that I was a meagre, poor, uneducated farm peasant? That I was without prospects?* Her brain, body and being were exhausted from the constant yo-yoing of her emotions. On top of that she was trying to cope with the daily manipulations of Malik's twisted mood swings. She felt like she was constantly walking on eggshells, never knowing what mood she would find him in. She was having to carefully navigate her reactions, trying to please him, trying to protect herself, but seemingly unable to ever do anything right according to her husband. She detested Malik with every fibre of her being. Moving slightly, she shifted her hefty bulk, trying to find a more comfortable position, the growing baby within her energetic, even the feeling of its little kicks unable to lift her dark mood today.

Her mind wandered back to their wedding day, of Malik smiling at her, the perfect husband, the perfect gentleman. His speech had been elaborate, embellishing their union, colourful and descriptive in his vision of them embarking on this magnificent new journey as husband and wife. He had spoken in detail of the life they were about to create together, raising a family, establishing their home. She had been surprised by his eloquence, a side to him that she had never seen, had equally admired how smart he had looked. His wedding attire had been elegant, the navy blue and gold brocade jacket sitting handsomely across his broad shoulders, opening to a long V revealing his pristine white shirt underneath, gold braid ornately embroidered, stitched down the middle of his shirt, white pants completing his look.

He had held her hand as he spoke, bringing it to his lips, kissing her fingers tenderly. The rupture of applause and cheers of congratulations was abundant from the family and friends that had surrounded them that day in the barn, cheers for this celebration, their union. The dark mood, a lingering sadness that had clouded her mind the morning of her wedding day, had lifted slightly, as she became caught up in the feverish excitement of the afternoon's celebrations. She had cautiously entertained the notion that maybe . . . just maybe . . . they could be happy together. Maybe she had been wrong about Malik. Perhaps their marriage could work. *Ignorant in the knowledge of what lay ahead for her,* she now scowled. Such fools. Everyone had been drawn in by Malik's false chivalry. She had been oblivious then but had quickly learnt that her husband was a master manipulator.

That night, their first time alone as husband and wife, she had been in the kitchen, looking around at what would be her new home, forcing herself to be as positive as she could, in her new circumstances. She was excited at the thought of arranging the layout of the furniture to her own satisfaction, making it homey for the two of them. Malik had been living in the house for a while on his own and, like most men, his housekeeping abilities had left a lot to be desired. But that was OK; she wasn't perturbed by the mess around her. She had been excited at the thought of getting started on the cleaning and giving the house a thorough going over. Malik had been quiet, but she wasn't unduly perturbed as Pappa was a man of few words . . . perhaps Malik was the same behind closed doors?

He'd taken his wedding garments off and changed into some loungewear which she couldn't help but note was very old and tattered, sinking himself into a dilapidated brown lounge chair, the hessian protruding from a large tear in the armrest. She had made a mental note to herself to patch the missing fabric over both his pant knees and the chair. She had been dismayed at the state of dilapidation of the house and furniture but had decided to be bright and positive about it; ideas had already started forming in her mind to replace certain items.

'Malik, it has been such a beautiful day,' she'd happily said, handing him an iced tea. Taking the glass from her without a word of thanks, he'd greedily gulped it down, liquid spilling out both sides of his mouth, dribbling down his chin. The atmosphere in the room had taken on a hostile feel—a chill, she had thought, Malik still non-verbal. Trying to initiate a conversation and create an ambience between them . . . it was, after all, their wedding night. She had gushed, 'That was a wonderful speech you gave, Malik.' She could hear her voice, sugary sweet, overcompensating. Smiling at him, she said, 'Everyone obviously thought so, gauging by the enthusiastic applause.'

There was a long pause between them. Then Malik said, 'You think so, do you?' The dull, harsh tone threaded through his response had caught her off guard.

She was perplexed by the course of direction the evening seemed to be taking, particularly after they'd had such an enjoyable day. 'That's a good idea, Malik, in changing. Think I'll follow suit and change into something more comfortable.' Her voice was almost melodious in her attempt to lift the dim mood it appeared Malik was in. Leaving the lounge room, she headed to the bedroom to remove her wedding dress, its brocade and multiple skirts weighing heavily on her petite frame. Struggling with the zip, she'd contorted her arm backward at an odd angle, deciding she didn't want to ask Malik for help. Alif suddenly entered her mind; she wondered what he was doing now, where he was. Performing her contortionist act as she tried to unzip the back of her dress, she'd quickly banished Alif to the basement of her mind, her longing for him too painful to allow it any space in her thoughts. To think of Alif would only conjure up memories that would serve her no purpose now. She still loved him deeply and a huge part of her still hoped he would come for her; but she was a married woman now and had to accept her position in life as her dear Jadda had reiterated that morning. Her back was toward the bedroom door, but she had sensed Malik entering, the quiet tread of his footsteps drawing to a halt behind her. She'd turned to face him, her dress dropping to the floor. She had felt perplexed at the look on his face. It was not the happy look of a groom just married. His behaviour had been out of sorts since they'd arrived at the house, and it was beginning to unnerve her.

Looking at him, she saw the smiling face he'd afforded their guests that afternoon was gone, replaced with an angry scowl, as if a lightswitch had been flicked. She had felt perplexed at his personality backflip. He was flexing his fists, which were held stiffly by his side, his dark scowl barely seeming to contain a rage. Her nerves were bristling from the uneasiness manifesting within the room, and goosebumps tingled along her arms and spine. She was now feeling quite frightened of him, confused as to why he was acting this way.

Without warning, he had grabbed her arm, shaking her furiously. 'Finish getting undressed, you little whore.' His whisper had been dark against her ear, as she stood there in her undergarments, the spittle flying from his mouth landing on her lip. Ironically, that had repulsed her the most at that point. She felt blindsided by his behaviour, taken completely by surprise after his perfect behaviour that afternoon.

'Malik, please, you are hurting me,' she'd lamented. 'What is your prob...'

Malik's arm had smashed across her face, silencing her protests instantly. Her tears had been rapid, the hot pain searing through her cheek before she could even finish her sentence. He had then started, like a demon possessed, ripping the rest of her undergarments off, with unguarded ferocity, the fabric shredding as he tore it from her body.

'Malik, stop, please.' Her voice was now high pitched, laced with terror and confusion. 'Please,' she'd begged. Holding her hands up to try and protect her face from any further blows, she'd been filled with terror and her cheek throbbed. She could feel it swelling. She'd lifted her fingers to her face, the thick stickiness of oozing blood connecting: the result of Malik's blow.

He had then pushed a footstool into the middle of the room. 'Stand on it,' he'd directed gruffly as he'd shoved her forward causing her to trip over the stool. 'You useless bitch, can't you follow a simple directive?' His boot had connected with her lower back just as she'd raised herself on all fours in an effort to stand up. The pain had seared through her back, his boot having connected a second time with her coccyx bone, causing her to fall flat again.

'I'll give you one more chance to get yourself upright and onto the stool,' he'd said, his gentle voice back again, his outstretched hand descending into her peripheral vision where she was on the floor, offering to help her up; his switch of tone confusing and scaring her.

'Malik, please,' she'd begged again. But before she could utter another word, the painful connection of his fist rained down across her face, splitting her lip, the metallic taste of blood filling her mouth. The gentle Malik of a second before was gone; dark Malik was back.

She'd stood upright on the tiny stool for three long, gruelling hours, the pain in her lower back searing through her like a hot knife through butter as she was subjected to his ridicule and cruel words, taunting and nasty.

'Ugly is as ugly does,' he'd mimicked repetitively in a high-pitched, deranged voice, as if in a trance, his manic behaviour terrorising her. She'd thought about trying to make a run for it when he had his eyes closed, chanting, but he was seated in the old armchair stationed next to the bedroom door.

'Consider yourself lucky that I've taken you on, for no other man would look twice at such an ugly body.' His words had been laced with venom; a repugnant grin had spread across his lips.

Hauling himself out of the low-lying armchair, his menacing stance just inches from her, he'd started snorting, long and deep, hocking phlegm up from the back of his throat and lungs, the sound utterly revolting, abhorrent. She'd had to try and contain herself from dry retching. With a long, deep breath, he'd fired his phlegm missile at her, the thick chunky mucus landing on the side of her face, its wet mass oozing down her neck. He'd stared at her, contempt in his eyes, and then, without a second look, he'd left the room. She'd tried hard not to cry, not to show any weakness, to hold in her pain, but it was to no avail. Her chest had been heavy, her throat constricting tight as the tears had started streaming down her face, her knees shaking uncontrollably. She could feel them starting to buckle under her from standing in the same position for so long; her calf muscles were contracting in pain. She could hear him in the bathroom, pissing, his stream loud, humming to himself. Everything about him disgusted her. She was shaking uncontrollably, fatigue overtaking her muscles. Tears, unstoppable now, streamed down her face. She felt overwhelming humiliation as she stood there naked, too terrified to move. Malik had re-entered the bedroom; his absence had only been brief.

Taking one look at her, in three short steps he'd strode over to the stool she was standing on. He'd halted within inches of her, their eyes directly in line with one another, their faces almost touching. She had been filled with terror of what was to come next, but daring to plead, hoping that she could somehow reach the nice Malik, she'd tried. 'Mailk, please.' She'd touched his hair tenderly, hating him, but hoping her tenderness would penetrate his manic brain. Without speaking, he'd gently placed one arm behind her knees. She collapsed into his embrace, his other arm behind her back, cradling her close against his chest.

Calmly walking to the bed, carrying her in his arms, he'd laid her down gently. His torso had hovered over the length of hers, their bodies nearly touching, his face directly above her. He'd stood there staring down at her for what seemed like infinity. She'd held her breath, unsure, not understanding this change in his temperament, his unexpected gesture of gentleness, or what to expect next. Time seemed to stand still at that moment, and hope filled her. But it had been short-lived. His eyes had taken on a beady look, the evil glint returning, filling her with panic, her heart palpitating rapidly. His presence above her felt menacing, his breath laboured. In one rapid movement he'd grabbed her ankles, his grip vice-like, and had flipped her over onto her stomach, before forcing himself upon her.

He'd thrusted angrily, grunting and panting like a wild beast, and his act seemed to go on interminably. She'd grabbed the bedspread, her knuckles clenched, white, the pain like a sharpened knife delving deep and precisely with each thrust. With a final grunt, he'd withdrawn, pushing her off the bed as if tossing aside a piece of garbage. She'd landed heavily on the wooden floorboards, the pain in her coccyx searing mercilessly on impact, ricocheting across her lower back. 'Piss off, whore,' he'd raged. 'A man needs his rest.' With that, he'd flopped his bulk of a body heavily onto the bed, splayed out, taking up the entirety of the area. Not needing to be told twice, she'd scampered, dragging her sore and wounded body to the lounge room and collapsed onto the couch, exhausted, battered and bruised.

The grey fog had landed on her that very first night. As the ugliness of her new reality had unfolded over the coming months, she had created a disconnection in her mind, the space calming, her safe haven of retreat, allowing her to detach.

She snapped her oppressed thoughts back to the present, Pappa still standing beside her, his arm draped over her shoulder, his invitation to talk hanging on the breeze like a delicate thread between them. A Chiffchaff nearby, raucous and sprightly suddenly takes flight garnering her attention. Momentarily startling her, her line of vision follows the small bird, emulous of the simplicity of its being. Wishing she could take flight as readily as the bird, her thoughts weigh heavily. She chews over Pappa's question in her mind. *Yes, I wanted to talk,* her brain screamed . . . the raging inferno burning within her head ready to combust. *I want to talk about why I was abandoned, sold out to this monster of a husband! You fell hook, line and sinker for Malik's act . . . promising the perfect husband, building a future together, creating a home! What were you thinking? Why, oh, why, Pappa, did you do this to me?* Her pent-up anger was intense, combustible. She could feel her veins bubbling along her temple, as if ready to erupt. But what was the point, she thought. Talking wouldn't change anything now. 'No', she answered instead, her voice little more than a husky whisper. *I don't want to talk Pappa. It is too late for words, for there are no words left to say.* Resignation was stamped in her brain.

She turned from Pappa, her heart like lead. She had started walking back toward the house, a half hour away, wanting nothing more than for her Pappa to envelope her in his big, strong arms, making everything right again, though she knew without a doubt that nothing would ever be right again, nothing would ever be the same again.

Half an hour later she entered the kitchen of the dump that was their home. It was a ramshackle old house that she had hoped to make a home on that very first day. She was greeted by Malik sitting at the kitchen table, his knife and fork in hand, waiting, baiting. His glare was accusing, censorious, his obvious annoyance palpable. 'Where have you been?' His foot tapped the table leg agitatedly. His body odour was strong, putrid; his tattered overalls were covered in camel shit; his hair was dirty, greasy, unkempt. Bile and repulsion rose in her throat at the sight of him.

'At the corral . . . with Pappa and Karim. The goats were performing. Karim is doing so well with them.' Her words tumbled out quickly, her anxiety heightening. Malik just sat there, unmoving, silent. She could feel the intensity of his mean eyes boring into her, his foot tapping growing in sound and beat. 'I see.' His eyebrow raised quizzically; his tone was low and menacing. The feeling of panic, dread and anxiety heightened within her, a constant state of being for her these days.

'And that's more important than ensuring my supper is on the table?' It was a double-edged question laced with venom. 'Of . . . of course not, Malik.' Her nerves splintered, like glass shattering in a window. 'It's only four o'clock in the afternoon—you never eat this early. I thought I had plenty of time to prioritise preparing a hearty meal for you,' she'd stammered. Her words were rambling, she knew it, but she was trying her best to placate him before he erupted.

'Are you questioning me, bitch?' She knew this conversation was entering dangerous territory and rule number one was to never, under any circumstances, answer the monster back. Another beating would be imminent: her 'REWARD'!

Her petrified thoughts were now on high alert. *Wasn't she the lucky one that he 'cared' enough to 'REWARD', beating her senselessly on a regular basis to help her remember her place in HIS household*? Oh, yes, Malik had drummed that into her time and time again. His physicality with her was his way of showing how much he treasured her, his adoring wife, his possession . . . and she had better not ever forget it! Time had stood still, as a rigid tension pulsated through the room. Malik's fingers drummed against the table, it's tone threatening, challenging. The ensuing silence seemed to drag on interminably, but in actual fact was probably only a matter of seconds before Malik spoke again.

'Do you want a beating, Yasmina?' His tone had become soft and gentle, as if he were offering her a holiday away somewhere, a choice: 'Do you want to go to the seaside, Yasmina? Do you want a beating, Yasmina?' The poisonous threat laced through his words sent a shiver of terror down her spine. Like a deer caught in headlights, she was frozen to the spot. His mood was menacing as he stalked her, his enjoyment of her discomfort evident by the smirk on his face. The steely glint of undisguised malevolence in his eyes unnerving, manic. 'Do you?' His tone had been quiet again, the tapping of his foot rhythmic, the beat crescendoing, in sync with his finger drumming, the tempo increasing, his dark eyes radiating a fierce, uncompromising evil.

'Do you?' he had asked again, gently, barely a whisper, justifying that by asking her he was inviting her to refuse, alleviating his conscience that a beating was what she wanted, knowing full well she had no choice of the outcome, so evil and twisted was his mind. She gulped; her throat constricted as she tried to swallow past the obstruction of terror lodged in her throat. Inwardly groaning, she winced as the stark admission hits her like a slap across the face. *I have failed the one job that I have been groomed my whole life to perform. To create a home, serve my husband. I have failed as a wife.* A despairing heaviness of futility settles on her weary body entombing her like a weighted blanket. As much as she tells herself that it's not her fault, she is unconvinced. Everything she does seems to irritate Malik ... her mere existence. Yet, when he is around other people he is a totally different person ... amicable, pleasant even. Suddenly she is so very tired of doing this on her own. She feels defeated. Her heart beat rapidly, fuelled with trepidation, plummeting into the pit of her stomach like an anchor freefalling into murky depths.

Her husband was a monster, despicable and rotten to his core, masquerading as a human being, and she is the only one that can see it.

CHAPTER 10

Elsie – Then

'Cheers, to freedom,' Elsie enthused, clinking glasses with Betsy, her identical twin. It was impossible for most people to tell them apart. 'My two English roses,' their father would say. They had straight blonde hair, the bluest of eyes, and long, shapely legs. 'You can thank your Viking forefathers for your attributes,' their mother would chirp. 'Unlike myself.' And it was true. Petite in stature, but not to be fooled with, their mother was formidable in every other way. She was not a woman to be crossed.

'Bets . . . a whole summer of freedom,' gushed Elsie, as they settled into the second week of their vacation. '. . . And so unexpected, which makes it even more delectable! No one to tell us what to do, when to do it, no deadlines. . . . Ahhh—divine. Life is deliciously good!' Lazing precariously on the chair's two back legs, Elsie raised her glass demonstrably. 'Saluti,' she said, before noisily gulping down her sparkling Pinot, simultaneously signalling Mario the waiter for another, winking flirtatiously at him as he approached. Mario, accommodatingly and without hesitation, efficiently approached, then reached across the table with the tray expertly balanced on his forearm to collect her fifth empty glass of the day—and it wasn't even 2 p.m. yet.

'For you, beautiful belle,' he said, his voice mellifluous. He smiled as he handed Elsie her fresh glass of wine.

'Grazi, Mario, you are the best,' Elsie purred, clumsily leaning across to where Betsy was seated, trying to chink her glass in salutation, but missing her target, wine sloshing over Betsy. 'Elsie, look what you've done,' Betsy chastised, aggrieved at her sister's carelessness, flicking her dripping hand backward and forward to air-dry it.

Elsie, dismissive, as if her sister hadn't spoken batted away Betsy's outburst, her dialogue inconsequential. 'How about we go for a swim after lunch Bets?', she suggested, her words slightly slurred. 'We can admire that dashing looking man we saw yesterday. Grrr, he made parts of me flutter that have never fluttered before,' she said, shuddering dramatically for full effect.

Betsy, playfully hitting her sister on the arm, her chastisement of a moment ago forgotten. 'I'll need to throw this bucket of ice over you if you don't calm down girl,' she laughed her voice teasing.

'Mmmmm, but Bets, you can't deny he *is* undeniably the Adonis.' Elsie dramatically emphasised the word *is*. 'I'll be his Aphrodite any day,' she purred. She was trying to be seductive, but a loud hiccupping noise unattractively escaped her lips.

Sighing, Betsy sipped her wine delicately, looking out over the picturesque beauty of the scenery before her. *My sister the maneater*, she thought. She felt sorry for this man, a stranger

Elsie had been ogling since their arrival. They were seated at a gorgeous little café owned by Mario's parents and Mario's father's parents before him. *And probably his grandfather's prior*, thought Betsy. The café was perched high on the clifftop overlooking the Amalfi Coast, the ambience of the location peace personified, the scenery before them spectacular. Interestingly though, thought Betsy, when she was chatting earlier with Mario as they both sat enjoying an espresso in his cafe's courtyard, he had explained to her how he would one day take over the running of the café.

'But don't you want to try something else, travel, explore, see the world?' she'd asked, bewildered. Unperturbed, Mario had explained, 'It is not for me to decide, bella. *La familia sempre al primo posoto*—family always first.' He seemed equally bewildered that one would want to pursue something other than their predetermined destiny. After they had finished their espresso's Mario had lingered at the table, as if he had something more to add, an indeterminate look clouding his face. His tone had seemed to allude to an air of ... what? Betsy couldn't quite put her finer on it? He'd fidgeted, twitching his lips, an unsurety in his demeanour. 'What is it Mario", she had asked. She could sense his uneasiness, but couldn't fathom what could possibly be causing his nervousness. 'Familia isa the mosta important thing ina the world bella. We musta always treasure ita dearly..... but it isa based ona more than justa love', his words blurt forward in a rapid fire, before he pauses to draw breath. 'There hasa to be respecta and consideration towards each other', his voice determined ... on point. Another pause, before a bashful look traverse his features. 'My apologies bella. I fear I havea overstepped the boundary of courtesy. It is nota my place to ... how do you say ... to be opinionated? So sorry if I havea made you feela discomforted?' His pitch a rising inflection at the end of his sentence, making his apology sound more like a question. He twists his cap through his hands, wringing it out as if he's doing the washing, an awkwardness sliding off him. Betsy gently raked her hands through her hair, calming it from the turbulence the afternoon breeze has wreaked as she absorbs Mario's words. She hadn't expected his outburst, his insightfulness. Organizing her thoughts, she pauses, aware he must be referencing Elsie. His words sound almost like a warning? What had Elsie done now, she wondered, to get Mario off-side? She looks up at Mario, not wishing for him to feel anymore uncomfortable than he obviously does. 'Thank you Mario', she offers. 'I am grateful for your words ... and concern'. She deliberates, is about to add that her sister has some ... ? Some what? She doesn't know? Elsie has always been ... well Elsie. Difficult, self-centered, egotistical... but decides against sharing her views with Mario - feeling bound by loyalty to her sister. She shrugs her shoulders instead, reaching across to Mario, laying her palm on his shoulder. 'Thank you for your thoughtfulness', and with a warm smile she rises from her chair and leaves.

Later the following evening, feeling luxuriously relaxed and lounging in the hammock, Elsie sipped a crisp, cold Chardonnay from the comfort of their rented villa, the quaint old building jutting from the side of the rugged clifftop, the breathtaking view of the Amalfi Coast spreading out beneath her. Moulding her body deep into the contours of the hammock, her thoughts reflected back over the events of the day.

She had dozed off at Guiseppe's bar earlier, basked in the late afternoon sunshine, grateful to Guiseppe for patching up her numerous cuts and scrapes. He'd diplomatically not asked questions, and she hadn't ventured into the origins of her injuries. The seductiveness of the coastal air combined with the hypnotic tunes of the quartet playing soft, romantic music at the restaurant next door had relaxed her mind, which was frazzled after the humiliation of her failed visit to 'the Adonis' earlier that afternoon. The music had lulled her senses into a sleepy state.

Guiseppe had awoken Elsie with a gentle shaking of her shoulder, suggesting it was time she ventured back to the villa. She'd sat upright, instantly feeling slightly disorientated, wiping the dampness she could feel from her chin, noting she'd obviously dribbled in her sleep and removing all traces of saliva with the back of her hand before Guiseppe discreetly handed her a napkin. *Oops, never mind*, she'd lightly chastised herself. Feigning nonchalance, she felt a giggle bubble up from her stomach. The sunny sound frolicked from her lips and everything around her suddenly took on a comical aspect in her inebriated state. The café had been near empty when she'd arrived, but looking around her, she noted it was now bustling, with late afternoon patrons filing in, readying for a full night of Italian music and festivities. The music from the restaurant next door was in full swing, the band's dolce voices filling the airwaves, eliciting a vibrant atmosphere. Guiseppe offered her his arm, helping elevate her out of the low-lying armchair in which she'd been sprawled, her legs splayed inelegantly as she'd stumbled, trying to right herself, mirth bubbling from within her again at how funny her situation seemed. Ever the gentleman, Guiseppe had kept his facial expression passive, but now, looking up at him as she endeavoured to upright herself, Elsie sensed an annoyance etched across his features.

Mario had been passing the café at the time, and Guiseppe, running his hands through his hair, beckoned Mario over to where they were now standing. Exasperated, Guiseppe's arms flapped about like a bird taking flight for the first time, irritation evident in his body language. Peals of laughter suddenly burst from deep within her at the sight of his bird impression. Her mood was buoyant; everything taking on a comical aspect.

Ignoring her outburst, Guiseppe peered beyond Elsie, his eyes darting across the dining room to the tall, willowy waitress who, with four customers gathered around her, was trying to attract his attention. He fired off a rapid dialogue in Italian to Mario, his tone clipped and the language beyond her limited capabilities to decipher, before handing her rather unceremoniously into Mario's arms. Guiseppe threw a harried *'arrivederci'* in her direction before hurriedly advancing to the waiting waitress whom she could see was now trying to pacify her disgruntled customers. *Poor Guiseppe*, she mused, as she watched the toe of his shoe clumsily catch on one of the uneven tiles in his haste, causing him to lose his balance. Unable to stop herself, and considering the scene before her ridiculously funny, Elsie laughed. The guffawing sound emanated from deep within her, loud snorts accompanying. It was most unladylike, she admonished herself. Guiseppe's over-correction of his slight trip reminded her of Manuel in *Fawlty Towers*. The more she laughed, the louder she was. Elsie was unable to contain her amusement over Manuel . . . no, wait, oops . . . Guiseppe.

Mario made a tut-tutting sound in Elsie's ear while linking his arm firmly under her, providing the upright support she found herself needing. Draping herself across Mario's broad shoulders, she was grateful for his physical support. Righting himself directly in front of the customer quartet, Guiseppe spoke, his voice carrying across to where Elsie was still standing. His tone was placating, overly enthused with charm, and it dampened the flames of their displeasure regarding their booking mix-up. Holding his arm out straight, he indicated for them to take a seat, and the two couples did so, while three waitresses frantically laid out fresh cutlery and glasses. 'Bravo,' Elsie called out loudly, clapping her hands together. 'Catastrophe averted. You are the best, Guiseppe,' approbation raining out in her voice across the room, her spaghetti legs exhibiting a little jig before they collapsed under her. Mario, indicating that it was time to leave, his grip on her tight, led Elsie out by the wooden side door, the patrons looking at them as she leaned heavily on him, her legs refusing to cooperate, seemingly having their own agenda at the moment.

They paused at the base of the long and winding rocky staircase, which led to their abode. Betsy had counted the steps on the first day they had arrived, merrily stating what a great workout this was going to be daily. 'Three hundred and twenty steps up and 320 steps down, Els,' she had enlightened her sister. *Six hundred and forty steps altogether every day*, Elsie thought. And that was the minimum as she doubted they would only traverse these steps once a day.

With that, Betsy had bounded up effortlessly, leaving Elsie at the bottom. It was with trepidation that she now looked up at the 320 steps looming before her. Her legs were feeling wobbly, and her balance was slightly off kilter. Mario had put his arm over her shoulder and under her opposite armpit, supporting her body weight. Elsie was most appreciative of this, and certainly let him know her appreciation with a show of planting a big kiss. She had been aiming for his lips, but with a swift turn of his head, he saw to it that the kiss landed on his cheek.

She'd draped her arms around him, turning her body so they were facing each other, pressing herself against him, feeling flirty, uninhibited, and trying again to plant another kiss, aiming for his lips. Laughing, she'd slipped her dress strap over her shoulder, the long, floaty silk material easily falling down to one side, showing her voluptuous cleavage. Mario had admonished her advances, disentangling her arms from his neck, repositioning her to his side. His voice stern, he'd reprimanded her, telling her she was lucky that his Francesca hadn't witnessed her display of ill-placed affection.

'You don't want to upset my Francesca. She's a fiery lady not to be messed with,' he'd warned. Laughingly, Elsie had batted away his warning and planted another kiss on his cheek. 'Bring it on,' she'd giggled, not appreciating his chastising tone or rebuttal of her flirtations.

'No more, Elsie.' Mario's voice had been serious now. 'Your behaviour is disrespectful,' he said, his rebuke clear. With that and in silence, they had slowly and steadily started their long trek up the 320 steps to the villa.

That had been several hours before. Now feeling refreshed and having ensured she'd hydrated herself once Mario had deposited her back at the villa, Elsie lazed back, luxuriating in the basking of the day's farewell. Looking out over their balcony at the expanse of ocean before her, she was captivated. The sight was spectacular, the sea glistening with myriad colours. The white caps were bobbing on the waves, looking like cotton wool; the sheer beauty of the scenery before her was mesmerizing. The sinking sun spectacularly heralded the end of another day, its rays a delectable feast of brilliant colours glowing orange, yellow, and vibrant pink—ostentatiously impressive. The sun, now a golden disc, was dropping rapidly, appearing to touch the sea's surface within minutes, seemingly in a hurry to end its day there, disappearing to go and enlighten another part of the world. It slipped behind the line of the horizon and the hypnotic scenery elicited in her a warm and fuzzy feeling. She realised her glass was empty of its delicious liquid, as she upended its delicate crystal rim against her lips, relishing every drop. It was a local vino she'd purchased from a cellar door. The winery's centuries-old building in the picturesque countryside wasn't far from the township and was quaint and inviting. Betsy and Elsie had ridden there several days before on bikes they'd borrowed and spent a few hours there enjoying a deliciously presented charcuterie board and pairing wines. Katerina, their host, had been entertaining and accommodating, knowledgeable and interesting. It had been a most pleasant afternoon.

Determining a refill was needed, Elsie called, 'Betsy!' then waited a few seconds, listening into the silence. No response. Twisting her head at an awkward angle so she was facing into the villa's roomy kitchen area behind her, simultaneously ensuring her voice was several octaves louder, she bellowed, 'Bets!' emphasizing her urgency. *Where was she when she needed her?*

'Bets!' she bellowed for the third time, her annoyance at her sister's lack of response now clear in her tone. She knew she was inside. Lorenzo from next door bobbed his head up, appearing over his miniature lemon tree hedge, his pots all aligned symmetrically across the balcony that bordered theirs. Her voice had obviously garnered his attention. *Nosy parker*, Elsie muttered under her breath, annoyed. 'Good evening, Lorenzo. Beautiful evening, isn't it?' she lilted in a singsong voice, directed at their neighbor. 'Everything all right?' she asked, pausing, then added, 'nothing to see here that is of your business,' hoping he'd get the message. His grasp of the English language was basic, so she wasn't sure if he'd understood, but he raised his hand at her in acknowledgement, a scowl on his face, before disappearing.

'Did you call me, Elsie?' Betsy said, appearing in the doorway. Her voice was breathless; her hair was wrapped in a towel, turban style.

'Oh, hello, Lorenzo,' she said, and waved at his back as he disappeared indoors. 'I was in the bathroom putting a treatment through my hair,' she told Elsie, facing her. 'I purchased this beautiful intense hair conditioner treatment pack in the market yesterday. Its scent is deliciously beautiful, completely herbal, infused with hibiscus, lavender and tulsi. Loretta from the apothecary recommended it. Oh . . . my . . . goodness, that little shop is divine. Loretta was telling me all about its history. . . . It's totally mesmerising. If only those walls could talk—what tales they could tell! I purchased some for you also, Els.' She paused for breath, smiling at her sister. Why does she always have to divulge so much detail with every verbal interaction, Elsie wondered, frustrated, not for the first time. She rolled her eyes in vexation while simultaneously fanning her wrist in a circular motion to indicate for Betsy to wrap up her monologue.

'OK, OK, OK, whatever. Thank you and all that, Bets, but can you please pour me another drink?' Elsie smiled, trying to hide her irritation, holding out her glass. Betsy pulled her silk robe forward where it had slipped off her shoulder, and Elsie heard the resignation of a sigh escape her sister's lips. Betsy walked across the stone tiled floor onto their geranium-laden balcony, reaching for her glass, a clouded look trespassing her eyes. Elsie hadn't meant to be short with her, but her sister's airy demeanour frustrated her more times than not. Betsy traipsed back into the kitchen with the empty glass without uttering another word.

Elsie could hear her clattering about, the refrigerator door closing firmly, but decided not to say anything. Several minutes later, her glass was replenished, courtesy of Betsy. Feeling relaxed, Elsie embraced the inebriated haziness of inertia beginning to fog her brain. Her body was tingling in a warm, fuzzy glow as she once again settled back into the comfortable contours of the hammock. Her thoughts wandered; she basked in the details of the earlier part of her afternoon—details of her escapades prior to going to Guiseppe's.

Elsie had spotted him sitting alone on a rocky outcrop farther down the beach that afternoon, his back turned, his head downward. She had decided to wander on over with the intention of making contact and introducing herself to the Adonis. Betsy had decided not to join her, preferring to retire to the villa, unexpectedly feeling malaise after lunch.

After doing some investigative snooping in the local village, Elsie had learned that his name was Alif, and that he was of middle eastern heritage. But any other details were sketchy and non-existent. Information about the new stranger was generally unknown. Elsie had clambered rather inelegantly over the rocks, cursing under her breath several times his choice of location, given the inconvenience its remoteness created for her. He hadn't turned once toward her direction during her advancement, which she had thought of as a tad rude, even though she'd loudly heralded her approaching presence, calling out 'Yoo-hoo, hello!' numerous times.

But she was not one to be deterred once she had set her mind on a mission. *Perhaps the wind had carried her voice in the opposite direction*, she thought. She cursed loudly this time as she scraped her ankle bone on a rock, and little blobs of blood immediately bubbled into a symmetrically aligned row. 'Bloody hell,' Elsie had cried out. Her expletive had obviously registered on the stranger's radar, as his body turned sharply to face her.

'Oh, hello, now you turn around when I've been calling out to you for the past number of minutes.' Her voice was contrived, annoyed, as her bloodied ankle was now throbbing. She began to question whether all the effort of the situation had in fact been warranted. 'Hello,' she said again, looking at him. Hello? That was it! Riled with annoyance at the stranger's lack of obvious appreciation of the effort she was making to reach his ridiculously difficult location of choice on this rocky outcrop, she'd stopped herself short of giving him a piece of her mind, instead consciously containing the descriptive expletives rampaging through her head.

Taking a deep breath and composing herself as best as she could, she ran her hands down the length of her short summer dress, straightening it after it had worked its way upward from all her rock clambering. Not that it necessarily bothered her, as she was confident in the knowledge of how stunning her legs looked. Extending her hand in greeting, she noticed at the last minute that she'd torn her fingernail. It was hanging jagged, also displaying a speck of blood alongside. 'Damn,' she muttered under her breath again, as she straightened her posture.

'Greetings. It is a pleasure to meet you. My name is Elsie.'

He hesitated, the time-lapse hanging in the air between them becoming awkward. 'Alif,' he said, and proffered his hand slowly, reluctantly. He clasped hers momentarily before withdrawing. His eyes roamed over her body, obvious.

'Are you alright? I see you have drawn blood.' He paused, before adding as if an afterthought, 'Forgive me if I am presumptuous in calling you *Miss*. He shrugged his shoulders slightly. His accent was strong, his voice rich and deep, pleasantly sending chills down her spine.

'On the contrary, the pleasure is definitely all mine,' she cooed, regaining her equilibrium and fluttering her eyelashes at him.

He had turned away, and his back was now facing her while he refocused his gaze on the ocean before him, seemingly lost in his own thoughts.

'So, what brings you to the Amalfi?' she ventured, not appreciating having to talk to his back. A disobliging silence once again stretched before them, and irritation started to infiltrate her mood. 'Are you always a man of few words when someone is trying to talk to you . . . Alif?' Her words hung in the airspace between them; annoyance at his indifference began to etch across her brow. *Shit, it was like drawing blood from a stone*, she mused.

With the use of his name, he turned, facing her. She noted his stare, which bordered on belligerence.

'You are presumptuous, Miss Elsie, that I am . . . how do you say . . . welcoming conversation. Quite the contrary.' He paused, seeming as if he was trying to compose himself. 'I come here for peace and solitude.' His words were drawn out, slow and deliberate; his tone was dark, an irascibility simmering under the surface. His rebuke had been obvious, taking her by surprise. She stood there, an uncertainty creeping into her confidence. She chewed it over, her mind tasting the rebuttal, this new concept unfamiliar to digest. She wasn't used to being dismissed by the opposite sex and didn't know quite how to react to his blatant brush-off.

She'd glazed her eyes appreciatively over the strong, muscled torso of the man standing before her, his creamy caramel-coloured skin glistening from his obvious recent swim, his dark hair curling in tendrils along the nape of his neck. Obviously, the Adonis's manners weren't as courteous as his looks, she surmised. Feeling somewhat rebuked, she turned to make her exit, not impressed with having to clamber back over the rugged rocks. The crashing sounds of the waves and raucous seagulls' cries filled the air, but with Alif's back to her, his silence was loud and clear.

'Well, it has been a pleasure to meet you, Alif,' she lied. There was no acknowledgment from the man on the rocky boulder.

As she made her way back to the shoreline, a large, greyish flecked crab with enormous beady eyes emerged from under its rock, shuffling sideways with surprising speed. Its unanticipated presence startled her, and the fright caused her to lose her balance. Instinctively, she veered her body at an angle to try and evade the crab's pathway. But she was unsuccessful, and her body veered laterally against an angular boulder, the side of her knee taking the full impact of her fall, connecting, scraping down the length of the rock during her descent. The pain caught in her throat, her breath raspy, registering the burning and stabbing sensation pulsating on her knee. She landed unceremoniously on her bottom in the wet sand between the two rock boulders. The crab was nowhere in sight, a fact about which she wasn't sure how she felt. Inspecting her knee with gently probing fingers, she was met with an infusion of pink and red; the jagged ripped skin lines were elongated like railway tracks, blood and fluid oozing.

'Jesus, I'll be like the walking wounded by the time I get back,' she cursed under her breath, grimacing with indignation at this new pain location. Without warning, tears started leaking from her eyes, thin rivulets running down her cheeks. She sat there momentarily, wedged between the two rocks, trying to regain her composure. Glancing back at the Adonis who was obviously oblivious to her distress, she noted that he wouldn't be coming to her aid anytime soon. She caught her breath before hauling herself upright and slowly continuing her clamber toward the sandy shoreline, feeling like a chastised child.

Struggling her way across the soft sand, hot underfoot from the sun's rays, she headed to Giuseppe's Café, ideally located on the beachfront a short distance from the rocky outcrop from which she'd emerged; her numerous cuts and scrapes heralded their painful existence with every step she took. Gratefully, Guiseppe's Café was relatively quiet, its outdoor courtyard sprinkled with a few patrons. She could hear their laughter and clinking of glasses, their Scottish accents easily identifiable. Elsie limped inside, welcoming the dimness and cooler atmosphere, and made her way to the right side of the room, making a beeline to the eclectic blend of mismatched chairs huddled against the herb wall. The wall, fashioned with an array of small terracotta pots anchored there by metal frames fabricated out of old bike spikes primitively engineered by Guiseppe himself, was an ingenious talking point with travelling patrons.

Choosing one of the overstuffed, low-lying armchairs, the green, gold, and black embroidered cushions plumped, she lowered her tall frame into it unceremoniously, trying not to knock any of her grazes or her head on a low-hanging pot. A waiter appeared, a young man. 'Ciao,' he said, acknowledging her with a wide smile. She snapped at him sharply, her fractured tone reflective of her diminished mood, and ordered a cold Chardonnay. He scuttled off, his beaming smile unmoved. Guiseppe appeared, parting the beaded glass curtains, their bright orange angles catching the flickers of light from the overhead bulb, clinking in unison as they fell together again.

'Mamma, mia bella,' he said, his eyes wide like saucers as he took in the sight of her. 'What happened to you?' He gesticulated with concern, waving his hands up and down her body in his flamboyantly expressive manner. 'I will fix you—do not move.' His voice was dramatic as if her situation was suddenly cataclysmic, and he scurried back through the clinking curtains, the tiny tintinnabulations eliciting a pretty sound, faint like Tinkerbell.

The sting of the antiseptic put her senses on high alert. Guiseppe dabbed effusively, tutting and clucking like a mother hen admonishing her to stay away from the rocks. 'It is your lucky day, bella,' he gushed. 'Lucky I am here, for I was supposed to go visit my sick cousin.' He paused his enthusiastic dabbing then, folding his hands in prayer whilst tilting his head toward the ceiling, eyes tightly closed, a penitent gesture. 'But he was too sick for a visit today,' he said, his accent thick with dramatic flair. Sitting quietly, Elsie settled back, relishing being looked after, appreciating Giuseppe's concern. Her body lapsed into a relaxed state once he had finished his first aid duties, and she downed her second glass of wine, the cool, refreshing liquid anaesthetizing the pain. She reflected on the afternoon's venture, her diminished mood bringing both feelings of irritation and a challenge wrapped into one bundle. Men did not say no to her; a vestige of doubt crept into her mind.

CHAPTER 11

Elsie – Then

A cacophony of sounds reverberated through the *mercati*. The markets, held weekly in the cobblestoned village, were filled with stallholders and people alike. 'Oh, I love it,' exuded Betsy, early Sunday morning, her eyes closed, breathing deeply, savouring the eclectic variety of smells. 'A smorgasbord of deliciousness—we really are spoilt for choice.' Elsie traipsed behind Betsy, her head throbbing like a beating drum. She'd rummaged through the antique closet in her room earlier, Betsy calling out insistently, 'Please do get a hurry on, Elsie.' She'd finally fished out her largest and darkest sunglasses, needing to mask the bold dark rings circling her eyes, her face masquerading as a panda bear. The puffy darkness was evidence of her big night before.

'Let's eat here,' Betsy declared, promptly halting her stride outside a brightly decorated wagon, her sudden halt causing Elsie to bump into the back of her. The wagon was stacked with an impressive array of pastries, invitingly displayed on the wooden counter benchtop fashioned out of a light-coloured wood running the length of the front of the wagon. Elsie's hungover mind couldn't help but admire the delectable array of products, the growl of her stomach agreeing and reminding her that she hadn't eaten since midday yesterday. '*Buongiorno, come stai. Il tuo cibo sembra delizioso,*' Betsy said, gesturing to the young girl behind the counter, her dialogue easy and fluent. '*Possiamo per favor sederci qui.*' She pointed to the tables and chairs arranged to the side of the wagon. Not wishing to converse, her need to sit down the greater priority, Elsie wandered around to the side of the wagon, knowing Betsy's conversation was going to be a long one. Betsy's girly voice, full of singsong and sweetness, reached Elsie's ears, her discussion with the wagon girl animated with laughter.

Elsie pushed the four flowerpots that were haphazardly arranged around the table's perimeter, each pot an abundant display of vibrant red geraniums, out of the way as she pulled out a shabby looking black-and-white wicker chair and gratefully sank her body into it. A red-and-white check tablecloth was draped over the table; another smaller arrangement of potted fresh flowers was staged in the centre. It was an inviting sight, Elsie quietly acknowledged. So very Italian. Italians presented hospitality well, invitingly. Elsie embraced the opportunity to sit down, pleased to finally be off her feet, having negotiated throngs of people and uneven cobblestones after following Betsy for the past ninety minutes. She sat enveloped in her thoughts, cataloguing the events of yesterday into some sort of clarification system.

Snapping out of her own reverie sometime later, Elsie realised she'd been waiting for what seemed a long time, tapping her fingers against the tabletop, her impatience starting to escalate as she waited for Betsy. Thirty minutes later, Betsy breezed over to Elsie, her cheeks flushed as if she'd just run a marathon, grasping the back of the chair, pulling it out from its position underneath the table. The chair looked even more dilapidated than the one Elsie sat in, with the unravelling of its wicker threads hanging randomly loose, its look unstable.

'Oh, Els, what a lovely girl. Her name is Catalina. Did you know her uncle owns this wagon?' It was a statement question. Elsie arched a brow at her, feigning interest, obviously not knowing that fact given that the wagon girl was a stranger to her . . . to them . . . but failing to point this out to Betsy.

'They rise at 4:30 every morning to bake all these marvellously delightful treats for the likes of us to enjoy,' she said, her sentence ending in a high pitch as if she'd just announced the cure for worldwide peace. Disinterested, Elsie changed the narrative, her loudly grumbling stomach dictating so. 'Are you ready to order?' Elsie again arched her eyebrow at her sister, affirming her question.

Before Betsy had a chance to answer, a familiar voice reached their ears. 'Ciao, bella,' trilled Mario, waving his hand. His greeting rode in over a sea of heads from the other side of the *mercati*. Mario bounded to where the women were seated. 'You likea *mercati*'? His question was a statement; he gestured with his free arm across the scene of stalls as he reached them beside the wagon. A large cane basket hung from his other arm laden with fresh produce and sourdough bread, jams and cheeses— obviously the labours of his morning endeavours.

'We love it,' Betsy cooed. 'There's such an amazing variety. A bit of everything, from pot plants to chocolate and everything in between. It's just so absolutely wonderful! You Italians are so welcoming to us outsiders,' she gushed.

'Ah, yes, my bella, the Italian hospitality, gathering together arounda fooda, the elixir of life here,' Mario said, the pride in his countrymen in his voice unmistakable. Betsy smiled broadly, and said, 'Please, Mario, would you like to join us?' She swept her hand to indicate the spare seat at their table. Elsie groaned inwardly at Betsy's invitation, her last interaction with Mario still fresh in her mind. Of all the breakfast guests currently on her 'to-dine-with' list, Mario would definitely scrape the bottom of the barrel. With the cold, hard daylight of sobriety registering the impropriety of her behaviour the night before, Elsie was uncomfortable in his company. Mario, obviously still annoyed at her behaviour, threw an accusing glare in her direction; however, Betsy, oblivious, insisted Mario join them. Wishing to be anywhere but there and not having to make conversation, Elsie grimaced.

'Oh, buck up, Els. Please do at least try to be civil and join in,' said Betsy pleasantly, her gentle rebuke surprising Elsie, who hadn't thought her displeasure was that obvious. Mario, feigning oblivion, pulled out the third decrepit wicker chair, half the bamboo seat having detached from its woven structure, and sat, gently placing his abundant basket by his side. Betsy handed them both a menu. Elsie fanned her face to alleviate the heat of the crowded space and then scanned the menu. Its well-worn pages were missing a substantial portion of its wording, erased from multitudes of hands holding it just as they were now doing. Admittedly, the pastries did look delightfully tempting and just what she needed to soak up the nausea twirling about in her stomach, a gift from yesterday's alcohol consumption.

Betsy took their order and approached the wagon counter to verbalise their requests. Mario and Elsie sat there looking at each other, neither venturing conversation. She noticed a muscle spasm in Mario's jaw and read it as vexation at her behaviour. Thankfully, Betsy returned efficiently and reinitiated conversation. Their dishes arrived and everyone began to eat. They were not disappointed, and, half an hour later, felt satiated.

'Mmmm, that was delicious,' Betsy said, licking the last of the custard off each finger. 'Such a credit to this hard-working family. I couldn't even entertain the idea of rising at 4:30 every morning—that's seven days a week.' Her voice boldly emphasised *every* and *seven days a week* in case they didn't register the profoundness of her statement. Mario enthusiastically agreed with her, flickers of icing sugar smattered across his face.

Everyone ordered a short black espresso, Elsie requesting a double shot in hers. The strong, bitter taste helped calm the vertigo dancing inside her head. She was grateful that her stomach had settled to a more stable state. 'You really were a cheeky little scamp, Mario,' Betsy had said after yet another rendition of the apparent childhood antics he used to get up to. Unintentionally, the boredom of the conversation elicited a yawn from Elsie, who cupped her mouth to hide it while Betsy kicked her under the table, connecting with the still raw scrape on her ankle from yesterday's rock-climbing expedition. She tried to contain her yelp of pain, covering it with a grimace.

'And what form of entertainment does your charismatic little village offer?' Elsie, feigning interest, asked Mario, silently grateful that he hadn't so far mentioned their previous encounter after she'd been banished from Guiseppe's Café.

'Actually, bella, nexta weeka is the beginning ofa the month-longa celebration of our patrona saint. Thisa year we are celebrating Sainta Maria. Ita will beginna with a procession.' Mario's evident excitement heightened his accent, and his words were drawn out, each sentence twice as long, which Elsie found irritating. Not to be rude, she tried to look interested, nodding appropriately.

'Father Joseph will leada the processiona througha the towna, altar boys following carrying the flaga bearing the symbol of Sainta Maria anda the community behinda the boys.' His face was flushed with excitement. 'It is an honoura to carrya the flaga behinda Father Joseph,' he finished.

'And did you ever experience that honour, Mario?' Betsy asked, genuinely interested and clapping her hands in delight.

'Si, bella, yesa, I did,' he said, grinning from ear to ear. 'Twicea!'

There was a short lull in the conversation then, Betsy smiling broadly, obviously absorbing Mario's enthusiasm. 'Pleasea, bellas, woulda you joina our procession nexta week?' His warm smile was generous as his dark eyes darted between the two. His invitation was genuine in his excitement, despite his displeasure in her.

'Perfect. Thank you, Mario, for your kind invitation. We'd be delighted,' Betsy answered excitedly on behalf of them both, clapping her hands again in glee. Elsie grimaced, a grunt of disdain escaping her lips. It was not what she'd had in mind as a form of entertainment.

'Perfecto,' Mario said, looking pleased. He rose from the table and gathered his overflowing basket into the crook of his arm, then bade farewell, explaining his need to get busy and back to his own café. 'Lotsa fresha pasta to make up,' he said, and Elsie grimaced again. 'Thanka you for your hospitality.' His voice was directed at Betsy. He dipped his cap and took his leave, though not before administering a dark frown in Elsie's direction.

'Yes, we must also head off, Mario,' Betsy said, speaking for both twins again. 'I have a macramé lesson at . . .' She paused to deliberate, nibbling at her lip, a muddled look crinkling her brow. 'I can't think of the name of the shop, but it's the adorable little stone building with all the arts and crafts in the next market square over.'

'Lucinda's,' Mario filled in.

'Yes, that's it.' Betsy's face lit up again. 'It will be enormous fun creating a work of art out of a bunch of knots. We are making dreamcatchers.' Elsie found her sister's last words amusing, and a giggle escaped her lips. 'That will be the perfect project for you, Bets.'

'What a wonderful morning it has been,' Betsy trilled as the pair walked along the winding clifftop path back to their villa half an hour later. Betsy had determined that she would walk Elsie home before partaking in her macrame lesson, declaring how dreadful her twin looked. 'A headache tablet and a lie-down are in order for you, Elsie, and I shall see to it that that is exactly what you get'. Her tone was frank, matter of fact. 'You look abominable'. She spoke as if she were Mummy, turning to wag her finger at Elsie for emphasis. Feeling chastised, Betsy's reproof certainly doing nothing to help her frame of mind, Elsie remained quiet. She lifted her opened palm, positioning it across her eyebrows, its spanse serving as a visor, shielding her eyes from the glaring shards of sunlight bouncing off the sea below. Concentrating on her footfall, Elsie was careful to tread with care along the perilous path. Betsy's singsong voice breezes through the airspace between them.

'Do be careful, Els,' Betsy chirped, as if reading her mind. 'This is dreadfully dangerous. We may perhaps need to write a letter to the local authorities about this stretch of path. It's a disaster waiting to happen. The saint's procession sounds exciting, doesn't it?'

Elsie darted a sideways glance at Betsy, whose voice was melodious about both the splendour of the upcoming saints' procession and rectifying a hazardous path. Betsy was the supreme optimist, unfailingly looking at the good in life and those around her through perpetually rose-coloured glasses. She had a sweetness about her—an endearing innocence, as others had put it. Over the years, people hadn't held back in stating their observations at how different they were in character, although identical in looks. There had been many times throughout their lives, Elsie recalled, when she had found Betsy's eternal optimism irritating—*very bloody irritating*. Surely it wasn't normal to be happy all the time, a querulous voice inside her head questioned. For all intents and purposes, it was *abnormal*, as far as Elsie was concerned.

Elsie groaned loudly, her thumping headache persisting in its thump, thump, thumping to its own death march tune. *Wonderful* wouldn't be her term for the long and boring morning she felt they had endured; however, she decided not to share her thoughts with her ever-positive sister. If this Sunday's church or saint procession or whatever it was supposed to be was the highlight of the entertainment around here, she thought, trudging behind Betsy's energetic step, *heaven help us*.

CHAPTER 12

Elsie – Then

Elsie woke up the following morning, feeling surprisingly refreshed. The headache tablet and lie-down the night before had obviously worked their magic, she acknowledged, pleased. It had been a while since she'd woken up without a head full of fog. She welcomed the gentle tones of 'Felicita' being played somewhere below, the notes dancing from a violin, floating through her open window, drifting in on the breeze, infiltrating the flowy, soft net curtains billowing into the room. She showered and washed her hair, using Betsy's hair products she'd purchased from the apothecary. She was appreciative of how her hair was left feeling luscious and perfumed. She wandered onto the balcony. Rosanna the housekeeper had obviously been in earlier, as a delectable array of croissants and fruit greeted her. The spread was laid out on lemon-coloured porcelain plateware, atop a crisp white linen tablecloth; a fresh pot of coffee was brewing on the hotplate. Betsy's dreamcatcher was hanging inside the doorway. It was her pièce-de-resistance, Elsie mused, wrinkling her nose at the ugly artwork.

The quietness of the house signified Betsy's absence, which suited Elsie fine. She had obviously gone out, granting Elsie some time alone to think, reflect and try to decipher what had been going on. Elsie poured a coffee. The rich aroma infiltrated her nostrils. She breathed it in deeply, letting it tantalise her tastebuds. Her thoughts wandered back a few weeks to just prior to their most unexpected vacation. It was the first time she could ever remember Betsy being downcast, out of sorts, and very much visibly upset. Her downcast mood had been concerning to say the least, and completely out of the realm of her normal happy character.

Elsie had tried to reach out to Betsy one evening when the two were home alone in the conservatory, relaxing after a refreshing swim as respite from the day's unseasonal heat, the chirping crickets heralding the balmy summer night. Elsie and her best friend Veronica had had plans for a day of pampering at the Spa-House followed by an evening at their favourite club, The Parading Peacock, but they had been dashed when Veronica and her boyfriend had a huge barney. The fight was in full swing, and a slinging match of pitched voices and nasty words rang through the barricade of her front door when Elsie had arrived to collect her friend. As Elsie had stood on Veronica's front porch, the fluorescent painted yellow door assaulting her eyes, a hesitancy of uncertainty had flickered through her mind as to whether to knock and interrupt or just turn around and leave. Not wishing to be the pawn in the middle of yet another of their melodramas, Elsie had left, knowing she would receive Veronica's hysterical call soon enough.

She had been annoyed when the phone's shrill ring half an hour later heralded Veronica's voice, tearful and wildly emotional on the other end, cancelling on her, yet again. Her continuous melodramatics since meeting this new boyfriend were wearing thin. So now, here Elsie was, trying to placate her distressed sister, the secret of her anguish irking her.

'Bets, whatever is wrong? You've been moping about these past two weeks. Surely nothing can be that dreadful in your sunny, coloured world?' Elsie had asked earnestly, genuinely concerned, seating herself beside Betsy, wrapping her arm around her shoulders. Betsy had looked at Elsie forlornly, her face pale and contorted, big, fat tears falling from her eyes.

Before she'd had a chance to answer, their attention had been diverted to the call of 'Knock, knock!' The friendly voice infiltrated from the direction of the conservatory's automatic sliding doors. Betsy quickly wiped away her tears and turned her head as Grannie Annie made her entrance. Scarlett, her pampered Pomeranian, scampered in, the red bows Grannie had lovingly placed throughout the dog's long, silky coat bobbing about as she pranced, first to Elsie, then to Betsy, in greeting, licking each of them enthusiastically.

'Hello, my poppets,' Grannie said, following Scarlett's line of entry. She embraced Elsie in a hearty hug before enveloping Betsy. 'Oh, my darling,' Grannie—who was not biologically related to the twins but had lived next door for as long as they could remember—said. 'My darlings,' she repeated, then comfortably headed to the bar to pour herself a glass of Pinot Grigio from the bottle resting in the ice bucket. 'How are you both? It seems so long since I've had the chance to visit. What with one thing or another and young Scarlett here keeping me on my toes, my goodness, there are barely enough hours in a day!'

Elsie raised her glass. 'Cheers to you, Grannie,' she beamed, knowing full well her elderly neighbour spent most of her day sitting in her armchair adoringly nursing her beloved Scarlett.

'My Johnathon is home again,' she announced, her hand on her heart. 'My boy is home.'

Elsie got up to refill her glass, bracing herself for another of Grannie's long, drawn-out stories. She asked Betsy if she would like a glass of wine, but didn't receive a response, before Grannie Annie's voice continued.

'My dear Johnathon is home again,' she reiterated. 'He's such a good boy and has so many new money-making ideas. Says he learnt a lot whilst away with study, was very educational, he says. 'Mark my words, Mummy,' he said very solemnly his first night home. 'This time, honestly, I will make you proud.'

Her 'good boy,' Johnathon, had recently been released from jail, having served time for being part of an illegal Bitcoin scam. Elsie could only imagine what he'd learned at his 'place of study,' as a guest of her majesty. At forty years of age, he was nothing more than a lazy con artist, Daddy had said, but of course she couldn't relay that to Grannie Annie, what with her Johnathon being the apple of her eye.

'Scarlett!' Grannie's high-pitched shriek reverberated around the room, startling them all, causing Elsie to spill her drink. Their eyes turned to the dog, who was busily digging in one of Mummy's kentia palm pots, soil flying in all directions, the dog disappearing more the deeper she dug. 'Scarlett, stop,' Grannie admonished again, her voice an octave higher this time as she lumbered her heavy frame to the pot, where she reached in and lifted the dog out.

Traffic of a Lie

'I'll have to bathe you again, you cheeky little scamp,' Grannie scolded, her tone light and loving, while she administered a big hug. Scarlett reciprocated, licking her owner's face enthusiastically, her squeaky barks echoing throughout the room. They were now both seated in the high-back French provincial armchair located next to the bar. Barely pausing for breath, Grannie's dialogue continued, singing the platitudes of her darling Johnathan. Elsie nodded in the appropriate places, masking her disdain for the conversation, but Betsy was non-interactive.

'Oh, poppet.' Grannie got up, gently resting the now sleeping Scarlett on the cushioned footrest nearby, and ambled over to Betsy, who hadn't said a word the whole while. 'Poppet, whatever is the matter, my angel?' She reached Betsy and enveloped her tiny frame, comfortingly pulling her into her ample bosom. 'You look like the cream the cat ate. Come, come, my darling,' she clucked like a mother hen whilst stroking Betsy's head. Elsie smiled at Grannie's idiomatic expression. She was always comically mixing her sayings up. Elsie was about to tell her it was 'the cat that got the cream,' and that being upset didn't warrant this saying, but she forgot all about it as Betsy suddenly erupted into gut-wrenching sobs, her body convulsing with each one.

Grannie looked over Betsy's head at Elsie, her brows arranged in a concerned manner. She was now seated on Betsy's other side, rubbing her back and trying to soothe her obvious distress. 'Betsy, sweetheart, please tell me what has you so terribly distraught,' Grannie whispered. 'You know a problem halved is a problem shared. Surely it can't be all that bad that you can't confide in your Grannie Annie?'

'She's been dreadfully dismal for a few weeks now, Grannie,' Elsie said, ignoring the butchered idiom. 'I've tried and tried to encourage her to open up to me, but she says she can't, and for me to be grateful that I don't know.' This, of course, had only fuelled her determination to know, she thought to herself.

'Oh, my goodness gracious, that is a worry then if you can't even confide in your sister, Betsy... most worrisome,' Grannie tutted, squeezing Betsy farther into her bosom. Betsy burst into another round of tears, gulping for air, her tears now melding with nasal mucous and the congealment cascading in a torrent down her chin. Elsie gasped, genuinely horrified at her sister's obvious pain, to say nothing of the snotty river running down her face. She had never seen her like this—something was evidently very wrong.

Elsie got up and went around to the front of Bets, kneeling before her, folding her hands into hers. 'Talk to me, please, Bets. You're scaring me,' she said, and wedged one of the thick, luxurious towels between them with the intention of eliminating any nostril liquid reaching her. Grannie Annie stood up and stepped back, allowing Elsie to access her sister more closely. The floodgates of tears had erupted again, and her body convulsed with big, gulping ugly sobs. She was truly alarming Elsie now. Her agonised sobs woke the sleeping Scarlett, and the little dog jumped up, barking enthusiastically at all the commotion. Grannie retrieved Scarlett and stood back. Elsie held Betsy for a while, patting her back, allowing her the time to regain her composure, unsure of what words of comfort to say.

The double doors silently glided open then, and the three of them simultaneously looked across the pool to see Mummy standing there. She was immaculately presented, as always, her hair freshly coiffured, her long, flowy dress elegantly swishing about her ankles as she paused at the doorway. A cold vibe seemed to enter with her, permeating the air, creating a chill as if an icy blast from the North Pole had blown in. Elsie noted Mummy's austere expression as she looked down at the scrambled soil spread across the entranceway. She didn't move, her beautiful features hard, as if she'd been taken by surprise, ambushed. Grannie went over, Scarlett tucked under her arm.

'Grace, how lovely to see you,' she said, embracing Mummy and air kissing each of her cheeks.

'Annie, what a surprise. I wasn't aware that you were here.' Her voice was contrived, not reciprocating Grannie's hug.

'I did knock at the front door, my dear, but, as there wasn't any answer, I took it upon myself and came around to the pool house, surmising I would most likely find the girls here. It's so delightful to see them both again.' Annie rushed her words out. Elsie could see Mummy bristle. She didn't appreciate unannounced visitors at the best of times, let alone now when something was so obviously amiss. Annie didn't appear to notice the tension.

'I do apologise, Grace, for Scarlett's mischievousness, the little rascal,' she said, referencing the scattered soil. As if on cue the little dog begins to yap excitedly. 'I would have cleaned it up but became sidetracked by sweet young Betsy's distress, she continued apologetically, raising her voice above the raucous of Scarlett's barking. Most upsetting. . . .' Annie made a forlorn face in Betsy's direction.

'If you don't mind, Annie, I wish for some time alone with my daughters,' Mummy said, batting away Annie's dialogue, her direct tone indicating she was without choice. 'I would be most appreciative if you could leave immediately, please.' Her words were firm, her tone brittle and hard. Annie appeared to be momentarily flustered, but Mummy's dismissal was non-negotiable. She pulled Scarlett in tighter in one arm, the dogs yapping escalating, before batting Betsy and Elsie a hesitant wave.

With Grannie Annie gone, a distinct hostility settled over the conservatory, the air rigid, uncomfortable. Betsy started to sob again. The atmosphere was awkward. Mother remained standing in the entranceway, her mouth crinkled in a tight line. Elsie could see a muscle tick in her jaw; her eyes were hard, as if she was surmising her next move, like an animal about to pounce, her daughters her prey. It was plain to see that she hadn't expected Annie to be there, her obvious annoyance masked across her face.

Elsie resumed her position beside Betsy, her arm over her shoulder, patting her comfortingly. Her sister looked a dreadful sight. Her face was swollen and blotchy from crying. Betsy, straightening her back, lifted her arm in alignment with her face, swiping her wrist lengthwise under her nose, trying to compose herself but failing, the arm on her skin now glistening. Elsie's stomach roiled.

'Everything alright, Betsy?' Mother's austere tone was brisk. It was certainly an odd question, when quite evidently everything *wasn't* alright, a critical voice in Elsie's head asserted, as she felt Betsy's body bristle under her touch at the sound of Mother's clipped tones.

Elsie shifted her position to kneel beside her sister, attempting to placate her rising hysterics once again. She looked up. The

Traffic of a Lie

last rays of the sun glinting on the conservatory walls gave the room an orange glow. The final vestiges of the day fragmented into glittering shards that bounced off the windows, the beauty outside a stark contradiction to the ugliness inside. Handing Betsy the corner of the towel, Elsie turned to face the other direction, feeling Betsy's hand brush against hers as she grasped it.

'Thank you,' she said, her manners prevailing even in her time of distress. She dabbed at her face and nose, sniffing loudly. Registering Mummy's voice, Betsy repositioned beside Elsie. She looked positively wretched. Elsie couldn't help but note that Betsy's face had taken on a manic appearance, an uneasiness settling into her darting eyes. Sitting fully upright now, Elsie let her arm slacken around Betsy's shoulder. As they separated, Elsie shuddered horrified at the sight of the silvery thread of mucus glistening in its attachment to her shoulder, stretching between them. *She obviously hadn't placed the towel adequately.*

'Bets, that is intolerably disgusting, disgusting, repulsive!', she shrieked, filled with revulsion, her skin crawling with repugnance. She knew her reaction was selfish and illogical, but she couldn't contain her disgust. Momentarily enveloped in her own distaste of the situation, she jumped backward in abject horror, the mucous link snapping between them.

'Grow up, Elsie.' Mummy's blunt tone speared into her histrionics. Startled, she looked up at Mummy's cold stare, which bored into her and Betsy from across the palms that stood fanning the doorway, like sentries on guard. Seemingly dismissing Elsie, Mummy focused her glare on Betsy, her dark eyes squinting, the skin around them deepening in her crinkles, her darkness speaking volumes without words.

Betsy, looking wild eyed, drew a deep breath, and jutted her chin out, a look of defiance firm across her jawline. Elsie was completely oblivious to what was going on between them, and the suspense irked her. Lobbing her head backward and forward between them, she stood up.

'What the hell is going on?' she bellowed. Annoyance skipped across her brow, her petulance fuelled by this feeling of being wronged, left out. How dare they?

Neither Mummy or Betsy responded to her outburst, the silence suggesting that it was determined to stay that way as they each stood glaring at one other for what seemed like an interminably long, awkward moment, as if speaking volumes without speech. The day had turned to night outside, the inky sky starting to twinkle with a few smatterings of stars. Mummy's eyes diverted upward, looking through the glass ceiling. She sucked in air through her teeth, a hissing sound emanating, before speaking. Her words were slow, deliberate. 'Betsy . . . my darling.' The 'my darling' sounded like an afterthought, her voice softening momentarily as if to appease the situation. 'Please compose yourself and then present in the study. I will meet you there in half an hour.'

Her last sentence, direct and precise, was delivered with authoritative conviction. Without another word, Mummy turned and left the room, her heels clacking noisily as she crossed the terracotta tiles, her dress recommencing its swishing motion in unison with her swaying hips.

Betsy sat down again, wiping her eyes before blowing her nose, the sound voluminous, filling the room. Elsie cringed but tried to be discreet, hiding the repulsion she could feel coiling through her stomach like a sickening parasite from the sound of her sister's loud nose blowing, sharply turning her head the other way. Once she'd finished, the crumpled tissues relegated to her shirt pockets, Betsy had stilled, as if collecting her thoughts, calming her quivering breath. Her demeanour was bereft of sound, her shoulders slumped in a defeatist pose, before she slowly turned to Elsie, her hushed voice one of pain.

'I'm sorry, Els. Believe me, you really are better off not knowing. Thank you for your support, I do appreciate it.' Her words were barely above a whisper as she wrung her hands together nervously. They had sat there quietly for a time, the airspace between them devoid of words. Not long after, Betsy also took her leave, squeezing Elsie's hand gently as she prepared to go face Mummy. A sadness hung in the space she'd vacated.

Betsy had exiled herself in her room for several weeks after that, refusing to interact with anyone. Eventually, she did rejoin the family unit, and returned to a semblance of her breezy, bright self. But Elsie could see it was a façade, that a despair and anguish that had never been there before were now attached to her sister's persona.

CHAPTER 13

Grace – Then

The vibe in the room had a prickly feeling after Grace dismissed Annie, who'd thrown a contrived look her way as she brushed past in her exit. Unfortunate. It had not been her intention to deliberately upset Annie; after all, she had been a relatively good surrogate grandmother to the girls all these years. She made a mental notation to endeavour to make amends later. *Perhaps I'll take her some flowers and a bottle of champagne*, she thought wearily. *I know she's partial to a drop of Dom Perignon.* That decided, Grace pushed it to the back of her mental *to-do* list, convinced she had more pressing matters on her mind.

She walked into the conservatory, where her pumps were met with dirt, the sound gritty underfoot. Annie's dog had obviously been digging in her pot plants again she noted, piqued at the mess that was strewn throughout the entrance. She cursed under her breath irritated, much preferring Annie leave her horrid little dog at home when she came to visit.

She paused just inside the doorway. A quietness had descended over the room, save for sobbing she could hear coming from

Betsy. She had expected only Betsy to be in the conservatory, having earlier conversed with Elsie regarding her afternoon plans. Elsie had indicated that she wouldn't be home until much later that evening. Hence, she was quite taken aback to see both Elsie and Betsy there. Annoyed at Elsie's presence she could feel a bristling web of irritation frowning across her brow ... she had been planning to have a private talk alone with Betsy.

Her mind skipped back to her conversation with Elsie that morning, positive in her recollection that she wasn't going to be home that evening. She had been in the kitchen enjoying a quiet moment, savouring the hot, strong, bitter taste of her English breakfast tea, when Elsie had bounded in, bubbling with excitement. She had been dolled up to the nines, her short, skimpy skirt leaving little to the imagination, evidenced as she leaned across the marble benchtop reaching for an apple. Grace had pointed out her daughters inappropriate dress attire, and her opinion had not been well received.

'Mummy, I'm twenty-two now,' Elsie had said, her voice dripping with belligerence, a critical stare thrust her mother's way. 'I certainly don't need your approval regarding my dress code.'

Leaving her snarly rebuke alone, Grace had enquired, what her plans for the day were and Elsie's snarl had instantly dissipated—such was the unpredictability of her moods. Grace rolled her eyes without commenting, as her daughter's mood pendulum swung back. Excitement lighting her eyes, Elsie had said, 'Veronica and I are planning a day of indulgence, starting with a spa treatment at André's.' Her voice was chirpy as she meticulously inspected the apple, affording it the attention of a quality control inspector. The tiny black spot on it evidently rendered it inedible, and Elsie had tossed the apple back into the bowl. André's was a favourite day spa the family frequented on a regular basis. 'Then tonight we're heading to the PP.' Her abbreviation referenced the Parading Peacock Jazz Club, a favourite amongst Elsie and her friends situated in the popular Soho district in the West End. Yes, she had definitely indicated she wouldn't be home. *I wonder what happened to change her plans?* Grace mused. *She wouldn't miss a night out on the town without good reason.*

So, seeing Elsie now in the conservatory, her arm draped around Betsy, threw Grace off guard. The two girls were huddled on the lounge together, the late afternoon sunlight skipping across the tops of their heads, creating a glistening halo of golden highlights. Grace stared at the pair of them, cringing at Elsie's pandering over her sister. She knew Elsie was trying to find out what was going on, and had been for the past few weeks, since Betsy had overheard Tomas and herself arguing. She stood stock still, gathering her thoughts, absorbing the differences of her two girls.

From a very young age Elsie had been a querulous and demanding child, exhibiting difficult behaviours, manipulative, self-centred, and egotistical—alarmingly so. Her refractory behaviour coupled with an insatiable appetite for getting her own way was exhausting. She had an attitude about her that even Hercules couldn't tackle. On the opposite end of the spectrum was Betsy, a delicate spirit, emotionally fragile, unable and ill-equipped to cope with the realities of life. She had been shadowed from blossoming under her sister's voluminous ego.

Tomas had always pandered to the girls' differences, protecting Betsy, keeping her distanced from the world, wrapping her in a cocoon of cotton wool so she didn't have to deal with reality, while simultaneously encouraging Elsie's sense of self-righteousness, proud of her 'independence,' as he had put it.

It was with horror that Tomas and Grace realised Betsy had overheard their argument, the heated ugliness of it all, that night. In hindsight, they realised, they should have been more discreet, professional, should have kept their business conversations contained to the office as had always been their plan, their number-one rule. But that night, emotions, ragged and raw, had flared, and disagreeable, atrocious words had been flung back and forth.

Grace had been in damage control ever since, she now thought sombrely. She had needed to ensure that the discussion Betsy had overheard stayed contained with just Betsy.... To have the information leak out would have catastrophic ramifications... for everyone. She knew she must now take charge, ensure damage control mode was a priority. *It is Betsy I must placate,* she thought. *Must make her understand. Tomas leaving it to me to fan the flames . . . or, more aptly, to put out the bloody inferno, while he left on a business trip.* With this thought in mind Grace steels herself, straightening her stance, rigid, feeling like a soldier about to go into battle. An overwhelming rush of frustration suddenly fills her. Frustration at always having to be decisive, steering the analytics of their business, have her finger on the pulse of so many variables at any one time. She's like a dancing marionette, being controlled by multitude strings. It only takes one string to snap and the integrity of all the others are compromised. Frustration at Tomas' incompetence and lack of business acumen clouds her mind. Pausing ... the intensity of her scathing thoughts take her by surprise. Their ascerbic honesty, which she now registers have been festering in her sub-conscious for some time, like an open wound, her conscious mind now suddenly ripping off the band-aid, blantantly exposing her raw truth. She acknowledges with her new found clarity, that her frustration is not isolated with only the short-comings of her husband, but extends to her two daughters. She churns this revelation over ... unsure of how she feels ... this is her family. But ... she can't deny the truth of her feelings. Frustration at Elsie's recalcitrant behaviour, the way it drains the energy source from her. Frustration at Betsy, always so timid, lacking strength of character, scared of her own shadow ... unable to cope with anything. Anything! The din in her head quietens as the realisation of these revelations slowly sink in. She pauses ... the pin-pricks of a migraine start to needle at her temples.

Taking a deep breath in, she refocuses, concentrating on tamping down the racing thoughts currently rampaging around her frazzled brain, Grace re-directs her attention to her daughters. Elsie had resumed her position beside Betsy, her arm looped over her sister's shoulder, her hand patting her. She felt the slight crinkle of a smile rise at the edges of her lips, tinged with a smidgeon of humour, noticing how Elsie had lodged a rolled towel between their faces. For all her toughness, Elsie completely unravelled at the sight of any sort of bodily excretions. One could not even blow one's nose around Elsie without her crumbling into hysterics. Betsy's current torrent of tears and subsequent nasal mucous would be abominably horrifying to her.

'Everything OK, Betsy?' Grace called across the room, a fatuous question when evidently everything was not ok, she had chided herself. Betsy rose, slowly. She looked wretched. A disheveled sight Grace noted as her daughter stood there glaring across the pool at her, her stare censorious, boring into her with undisguised hostility. She cringes under the intensity of Betsy's stare; it's a side to her daughter that she has never witnessed. *Maybe Betsy is finally growing a backbone,* she thinks with admiration. Elsie suddenly screams, snapping the tension that is strung like a tight-rope between Grace and Betsy, re-directing their attention. Her strident cry is dramatic, her theatrics more worthy of an Oscar nomination Grace thinks sourly. Unable to contain her ascerbic tone, a reflection of her diminished mood, Grace admonishes Elsie's histrionics, whilst summoning Betsy to meet her in the study in half an hour. She has had enough of the pair of them. Turning on her heel, she leaves the room.

CHAPTER 14

Elsie - Then

The following Sunday provided cooler weather but the unexpected drop in temperature certainly wasn't dampening the festive vibe permeating the procession, thought Betsy, as she walked alongside Mario toward the rear of the group. They had left at eight that morning, the large gathering led by Father Joseph was followed by the altar boys, each of them bedecked in long robes of various colours, rich and vibrant. Their young faces were scrupulously scrubbed, their hair shining, several proudly leading the entourage carrying between them an intricate and elaborately embroidered flag depicting St. Maria. The flag billowed out on the breath of the wind. Betsy had marvelled at the virtues of the woman, saintly by all accounts, only a child at the time, who had been savagely murdered for resisting an attack on her chastity, and was now the patron saint symbolizing purity, rape victims, young women, and youth in general. It was admirable in an era when being of a different opinion took strength, courage and determination. Elsie traipsed several steps behind, engrossed in her own thoughts, Betsy's voice droning on as she praised the merits of St. Maria, the details washing over her indifferently.

She had visited the local taverna the night before, alone. Betsy had not been interested in accompanying her. 'You know taverns aren't my style,' Betsy had announced, arms gesticulating as if to emphasise her point. 'Plus, I'm deeply engrossed in this amazing saint we're paying our respects to tomorrow. You should read about it yourself, Els! Most intriguing.'

Elsie couldn't think of anything more boring than staying indoors on a beautiful evening on the Amalfi Coast reading about a long-dead saint. 'Suit yourself,' she had replied, not perturbed by whether Betsy accompanied her or not.

Later that evening, wearing a knowing confidence that she looked good after spending the afternoon styling her hair and nails, her white lace Dior dress perfectly accentuating her curves, Elsie had left the villa. Navigating the cobblestoned streets in her high heels, an accomplishment in itself, she'd ventured toward the village square, eventually sighting and entering the dimly lit tavern that had been recommended to her by Louis from the fruit and vegetable market.

Upon entering, she was pleasantly surprised that the tastefully designed décor instantly created a welcoming and seductive atmosphere, its ambience eliciting a moody vibe. A pianist was located in the middle of the floor on a slightly elevated platform. His fingers glided effortlessly across the ivory keys, his harmonious tunes and euphonious songs creating a melodic harmony. Elsie flipped him a wink as she passed by, heading to an empty booth toward the rear of the room. Admiration filled her. She was appreciative of the classical décor, from the mahogany-lined walls to the booth seats. Each seat was adorned in an intricate pattern, the woven brocade heavily embroidered, gilt-edged cushions scattered throughout. The interior had taken her by surprise. The building and decor were incongruous with the eclectic casual buildings featured throughout the small village.

Folding her lace dress under her legs, Elsie eased herself into the sumptuous booth. The waiter arrived efficiently, delicately placing before her the glass of Shiraz she'd ordered on her way past the bar. He hovered momentarily, before delving into an in-depth monologue about the local history and virtues of said red wine. Elsie was disinterested in hearing his spiel and wished he would leave her in peace. She sat fidgeting while his voice droned on, hoping he'd register her disinterest, rather than her having to ask him to leave. She yawned loudly then took her first sip, savouring and swishing the sweet nectar around her mouth. The flavour was rich with depth, easy on the palate.

Gratefully, it wasn't long before the waiter was beckoned by another patron. He excused himself and took his leave. Elsie moulded her back comfortably into the cushion behind her, melding luxuriously into the ambience of the room. The soft tunes emanating from the ivory keys began to lull her senses into a state of relaxation. Her eyes strolled around the room, absorbing her surroundings. She sat there, enjoying the tranquilizing effect the wine and the music soon began to engender. She noted the young couple seated in a booth a short distance from her. The woman had rich, long dark hair, a voluptuous figure, and brightly embellished red lips that smiled at the man sitting opposite. They held hands, the two of them, blissfully ignorant of anyone else, their gazes for each other only. Three booths over, sounding like a gaggle of galahs, seven women chatted animatedly, each voice one octave higher, talking over each other. Their infectious laughter and clinking glasses sounded across the room. The ease with which they interacted suggested a long friendship over which Elsie mulled. Perhaps it was a friendship navigated through laughter, tears, arguments, agreements, and disagreements amid the myriad other entanglements that make up longstanding friendships, she mused.

As Elsie sipped her third glass of wine, a high-pitched screech, a sound akin to fingernails being dragged down a chalkboard, heralded the opening of the tavern's front door. The doorway needed some serious maintenance she thought as she peered across the dim room, its cloudiness now a thick haze of cigar smoke. The mood was seductive, the voices subdued, romanticism blending and swaying with the pianist's ivory tinkling. A frisson of excitement sizzled down her spine as she spied 'the Adonis,' his presence there that evening an unexpected bonus. He was standing in the doorway, looking delectably delicious, casually dressed, his style meticulous. A girlish churn languished within Elsie, an unpredictable excitement bubbling. The evening was suddenly looking more enticing.

She raised her hand to attract his attention. Her bangles tinkled with her movement. He appeared to be looking directly at her, but was seemingly oblivious to her welcoming gesture, as he stood unmoved in the doorway. She waved again, tinkling, before a whisper of remembrance threaded through her mind, detailing their recent unpleasant encounter on the beach. Uncomfortable in the memory, she lowered her hand, deliberating her next move. She decided to sit quietly for a moment and observe instead.

He stood there for what seemed an indeterminate length of time, the hot air outside infiltrating through the open doorway. The waiter, whom she now knew was named Francis, indicated a table close by, a wide, welcoming smile plastered across his face, flashing his pearly white teeth. The Adonis hesitated before following Francis's arm, then moved slowly to take the seat offered to him. Elsie couldn't help but notice his dour body language, the same forlorn look about him as the other day, snippets of their last awkward meeting drip feeding through her mind.

He seated himself, his shoulders slumped. Francis re-appeared by his table and placed a drink before him. Elsie watched Francis, smiling at his latest customer, his lips moving, speaking for quite some time, his words indeterminate to her from her distance. The Adonis nodded before resuming his slumped position. With a nod of his head, Francis turned, his sprightly step at odds with the slow ambience of the room as he sprang forth to attend to other patrons. Elsie bristled, a feeling of indignation washing through her. The Adonis's selfish demeanour was inexplicably irritating to her, and it dented her buoyant mood. She had come there for a bit of fun, not to have her good mood dampened by Adonis doldrums.

She sat and observed for a while before deciding to rectify the situation. She summoned Francis and he appeared instantly to take her order of two glasses of his best wine, indicating that one of them should be delivered to another table. Feeling flirtatious, she reclined into the embrace of her cushion, watching and waiting for her opportunity to arrive.

CHAPTER 15

Alif – Then

Alif pulled the front door of his villa behind him, the latch of the patchy, paint-peeling red door firmly locking, heralding a large clunk, an encouraging sound. If only, he thought, he could silence the torturous voices in his head that easily. The need to get away from the confines of his villa and the lecherous demons constantly battling inside his head had propelled him out the door. He sought people, crowds, the sounds of life, normality, hoping they would anchor him to the present, even though he had no desire to interact with these sounds. The last few hours, alone inside his head, had initiated a sizeable headache. He groaned and massaged his throbbing temples.

The late heat of the day greeted him unapologetically, the glare of the bright afternoon sun rays blinding as he set off at a casual stroll along the cobblestone streets. He was unable to offer the beauty of the region the justice it deserved; his mind unable to function normally these days. The ancient structures, magnificent history, and charming terraced orchards were all squandered on his inability to appreciate anything, anymore. He was attuned to the volume of people around him as they embraced this pleasant Saturday evening, laughing, chatting, and happily interacting—normal human behaviour that was now beyond his scope. He trudged past numerous couples, each strolling hand in hand, hearing snippets of their jovial conversations as they passed, the contrast highlighting all he'd lost.

He ventured down into yet another alleyway, wandering its length, meandering out the other end and finding himself in the village square. The inviting timbre of a piano emanated from the taverna, the building situated a few metres beyond an elaborate, gold-edged fountain located a short distance along the cobbled area before him. He breathed in the beauty of the music, the notes enticing him toward it as the piano evoked memories of Mamma. *She used to play so beautifully*, he recalled wistfully, then immediately pushed the thought into the recesses of his mind. *Thinking of Mamma will serve me no purpose*, he chided.

He swung open the heavy wooden door of the taverna, and a dim haziness greeted him. The dark interior suited his purpose perfectly. It took a moment for Alif's eyes to adjust to the subdued lighting. When they did, he registered a hand waving at him through the clouds of smoke. He stared across the room, thinking the wave must be directed at someone else, for he had purposely not allied with any comrades since arriving. It then struck him that the waving hand was that of Elsie, the infuriating woman who had accosted him on the beach the other day.

Instantly feeling deflated, he debated leaving, having neither the stomach nor the inclination to interact with that irksome woman again. Just as he was about to make his departure, a waiter approached, his greeting welcoming, and gestured for him to take a seat at a vacant table nearby. Deliberating, not wishing to be alone with his own fractured thoughts again, Alif hesitated regarding his next move. Deciding to stay, he accepted the waiter's invitation.

He sat there with his gin and tonic in hand, allowing the ambience of the tavern to divert his attention from his problems. The waiter, Francis, was a wealth of knowledge and an interesting conversationalist, articulate on a broad range of topics. Alif allowed him the airspace between them, happy for him to steer the conversation, expecting minimal input from him. He listened with interest, grateful for the diversion from his own current morbid mindset. After the waiter left Alif to attend to other patrons, he was left with the company of his own thoughts again. They sank deeply and swiftly into the gravity of his situation and sat heavy on his heart like a lead balloon.

So engulfed was he in his thoughts, oblivious to his surroundings, Alif was startled out of his reverie as Francis appeared before him again. His eyes darted sideways as he placed a glass of red wine before Alif. Slowly turning in the direction referenced by Francis, his eyes landed on Elsie. An instant horripilation of annoyance rippled along his arms.

Elsie was seated in a booth at the rear, some four tables away. Undoubtedly the woman was looking elegant, he reluctantly acknowledged, her long legs crossed, unashamedly on display, her dress too short to cover them. Alif could see her eyes glistening, detecting a hint of suggestion contained within. She raised her glass toward him, self-assured. Breathing deeply, infinitely frustrated, he reciprocated, raising his glass in acknowledgment of her gesture—rudeness was not his fortitude. This woman was everywhere, he thought, turning away from her, hoping she would take the hint and leave him alone now.

She didn't and, seconds later, he heard her voice behind him. 'A gentleman shouldn't drink alone,' she said, her voice satin and seductive. 'Mind if I join you?' she asked. But it was more a statement than a question. He'd never met a more presumptuous woman. Not waiting for an answer, she gathered up her purse, and, with wine in hand, her gait slow, her hips swaying, she sauntered to his table.

'Thank you for the invitation to join you,' she purred. Balking at her arrogance, *her audaciousness was mind boggling,* he turned away from her. Her interpretation of the actuality of the situation annoyed him. Reaching out, her hand on the back of the chair opposite him, she was jolted by the weight of the chair as she tried to manoeuvre it backward to seat herself. The jolt from the unexpected weight caused her drink to spill over her hand, splashing onto the white lace of her sleeve.

'Damn,' she said, and her annoyance was evident as she watched the stain spreading pink on the sleeve. Her seductive veil slipped from grace as she glowered menacingly, directed at him, her annoyance obvious. Forgetting herself, *apparently the spill was his fault due to his obvious lack of social graces in failing to rise and pull the chair out for her . . . no less than what any gentleman would do, particularly after her peace offering of buying him a drink and gracing him with her company.* She berated him, her voice laced with dramatic flair, her embarrassing outburst garnering the attention of other patrons.

Alif's aura of ungratefulness was apparently unbecoming and unattractive. But he was not perturbed by her fractious outburst and made no attempt to move from his position. *Not my monkey, not my circus*, he thought, ignoring her, wishing she would leave him alone. Alerted to all the commotion, Francis came loping across the room, a wet cloth in hand, and dabbed at her sleeve to soak up the wine stain, failing. He bounded back to the bar, an air of urgency in his stride, as if the need to placate the distressed damsel was of utter importance. He returned with a fresh complimentary glass of wine. This gesture seemed to appease the woman, who was now quietly seated beside Alif.

'What's a handsome man like you doing alone in such a beautiful and romantic location?' she asked, each syllable strung out in a soft drawl, a suggestive utterance purring off each word. Composed again after her outburst moments before, Elsie draped her arm across the table, running a red manicured finger along his arm. Ignoring her question, Alif removed his arm from her reach, a tremor of annoyance rippling down his spine. His frustration with the audaciousness of this woman was compounding his already melancholic mood. He considered her ineptness at recognising personal boundaries reprehensible. Annoyingly so.

She stared at him, as if calculating her next move, like a cat on the prowl, an expression of incredulity across her face. He sat there, weighing his options, thinking he should leave the taverna and remove himself from this woman's manipulative presence, whilst knowing he probably wouldn't. His mind charged into a one-man battle, weighing up the pros and cons. The idea of returning to the four walls of his villa, alone, caged within the dark turbulence of his mind, being at the mercy of the blackness of his subconscious, was a more dire prospect to him than staying there.

Alif snapped back to the present, the click of Elsie's fingers grounding him, insouciantly, her hand held directly above her head, summoning Francis over. Without hesitation, Francis was by her side, as if appearing out of thin air, efficiently at the ready. Her self-righteous voice bleated, 'Another two of your finest reds. Nothing but the best for my sad little friend here.' She tactlessly referenced Alif with a swish of her head, her lips curling into a smile, as if it was all a game to her, as she looked up at Francis. Alif's blood boiled at the audacity of this belligerent woman and her self-righteous, passive-aggressive behaviour. Perhaps, warring within his head was the better option, he thought, his own demons being more favourable. He began pushing his chair back, readying to rise. Elsie's voice butted in: 'What is your favourite flower, Alif?'

The random question came at him from across the table, halting his ascent out of his chair mid-air. He paused, looking at her quizzically. 'A person's choice of flower can speak volumes about their character.' The statement was delivered matter-of-factly. Alif paused, unsure of her game tactic, Francis placing another wine in front of him, courtesy of Elsie, unappreciated by him. He fussed about, methodically arranging an assortment of brightly decorated small bowls containing pistachios, olives and crostini before them, apparently complimentary.

'Well?' Elsie, her perfectly arched eyebrow, a triangle in the middle, focused on him, obviously waiting an answer. Alif found himself unexpectedly interested in where her line of question was leading. 'Actually, I'm not a flower person,' he responded, his mind flashing back to his mother's funeral, which had been laden with an exorbitant volume of flowers everywhere, as he eased himself back into the contours of the velour-clad chair he'd partially vacated. 'I prefer to focus on more sustainable plants,' he said.

A sense of rivalry overcame him then. He wanted to outsmart her and wipe her grin, spread full of smugness, like a cheshire cat, from her face.

'Admirable,' she responded, nibbling on the corner of her lip as if churning over his statement. 'But everyone has a flower within them.' She stared at him momentarily, her glare unnerving, before speaking.

'I see a black dahlia in you, Alif. Your aura exudes a darkness.' With that, she delicately placed her hand on his. He withdrew his hand from under hers.

'A black dahlia is like the devil in disguise. It looks beautiful, drawing one in with its beauty, its uniqueness.' Her voice had lowered as she leaned across the table closer to him, the music and din of voices around them fading into the background. 'Fooling innocent people, making them delight in their presence.' He shifted in his seat, the context of her monologue sitting awkwardly with him. 'And once they have you beguiled, firmly within their clutches, they betray those that have fallen in love with them. They are an evil and dishonest flower.'

She tilted her head, a conniving smile spreading across her face as if she'd played the upper hand, her trump card, letting the last sentence linger between them. He was thrown off balance by the accuracy of her interpretative insight, his fingers drumming against his leg under the table.

A burst of song erupted from the table of women close by, snapping the thread of tension stretched heavily across their table. Elsie threw her head back effusively, animatedly clapping, turning to cheer the women on. She threw a glance across to him, laughing loudly above the loud, out-of-tune-voices. 'You should have seen your face, Alif! Did I hit a nerve? A bit too accurate, maybe?'

Popping an olive into his mouth, he shifted uneasily, the acrid taste of her words of prediction rolling around, blending with the saltiness of the olive, neither sitting comfortably with him.

Sometime later, Elsie said, 'You had to be there!' Her raucous laugh reverberated loudly, tiny spittle leaving her lips. She playfully punched Alif's arm, an overtly familiar gesture he did not appreciate. Several hours had passed since her unnerving flower revelation, and her alcohol consumption over the course of the night was significantly taking its toll, as her decorum rapidly declined. Her inebriated rowdy behaviour was most unbecoming.

Several other patrons had joined their table, Elsie's pantomime performance enticing them over, her revelling in having an audience. Another woman approached the small group now congregated at the table, her Amazonian height and stature coupled with her bright red hair and equally bright red dress ensuring she was an unmissable sight. Elsie looked up, sharply stopping mid-sentence from her elaborate rendition of 'God Save the Queen,' a 'crown' on her head fashioned from several serviettes and a few hairclips that held her ensemble in place, albeit askew, on her head. 'Welcome, welcome, welcome, girlfriend,' she enthused loudly, gesticulating with her arm, waving it in a haphazard circular motion propositioning for the red lady to join the table amidst the numerous others. The woman, 'Genevieve,' apparently, embraced Elsie enthusiastically, the two of them acting like best friends thirty seconds into making one another's acquaintance. The newcomer excitedly patted Elsie on the back; her vigorous patting action caused Elsie to spray her mouthful of wine fountain-like across the table. Hysterical laughter erupted between the two of them.

'Y'all so funny,' Genevieve said, an obvious Texan twang drawing out her sentence, her nasally voice loud. The brash behaviour of the two of them disgusted Alif. Elsie's frivolous anecdotes of past experiences bored him in their entirety. Alif's thoughts turned inward, reflectively, Elsie's voice droning into the background, her one-person-show holding court, so comfortable was she being the centre of attention, her audience eating out of her hand, hanging onto her every word. Genevieve's deep, nasally voice invaded his mindset, coming at him from a distance encouraging her newfound friend's behaviour at every opportunity. Contemplatively, he rubbed his hand across his chin, zoning out from the circus around him, the fleeting thought of another lady who used to love the prickly feel of his face fluttering across his memory, its visit grabbing a miniscule of a second before he pushed it back down deep into his well of not-to-go-to places, archived, where it needed to be.

He could feel his mind free-falling, a state of panic starting to overwhelm him. Clenching his fists, he willed his mind not to go there, not to detour to its place of pain and suffering, the raucous background noise around him fading into the distance, a vacuum of black starting to release its tentacles, its grip tightening. *Please, please, please, not here, not now*, he begged, trying to shut it out, to rebuke the demon.

But, to no avail, the Depression knocked loudly on the inside of his eyelids, its insidiousness determined, negative to being silenced. Alif could feel the Black Beast, demonic, heralding its arrival with intensity. It was destructive, belligerent, debilitating. His constant uninvited companion, always close by, lingering just under the fragile surface of his false facade, flaring up again like a beacon in the night sky, swift and unannounced. Flexing its muscles, ready to initiate combat, its darkness slowly twisting and turning, through his lifeblood, crushing, synchronising each compression in beat with Elsie's raucous squawking in the distance.

The beast didn't care if he had an 'episode' in the company of others. It didn't differentiate the logistics of how and when. Breathing deeply, concentrating profoundly, he tried his uttermost to hold it at bay, to ward off its evil clutches. Elsie's high-pitched shrieks reached his ears, her cackles tainted with self-righteous indulgence, distant, as though travelling through a vacuum, piercing, the chords akin to razor talons mercilessly shredding at the inside of his skull. The demon was unravelling him—he knew it. He could feel it. He couldn't stop it. Dr. Yassouf came to his mind again, his suggested coping strategies still eluding him, his panic escalating rapidly.

Grateful, ironically, Alif almost laughed to himself, or maybe he did laugh out loud, judging by Genevieve's strange stare. His hysteria was building. He was euphoric in the realization that Elsie's behaviour, her self-centred, egotistical, attention-seeking, one-person pantomime show that she was delivering with such animated relish, as much as it was to his distaste, was in fact ensuring the crowd's attention, the numbers congregated around their table having grown over the past hour, all solely focused on her, not him. He was invisible to them—or so he hoped. *I need to get away*, he realised, his laboured breathing becoming more acute.

And so, he did, unnoticed, without saying goodbye. He was grateful that the self-centred Elsie seated next to him was oblivious to his distress. He pushed away her leg that she had draped familiarly, unwelcomingly, over his knee, suggestively under the table, so enraptured was she in her own being. Alif discreetly vacated the premises, leaving that woman to entertain her audience, oblivious to his departure.

CHAPTER 16

Alif - Then

Exhausted from his fractured night, Alif had come to his place of peace. After leaving the taverna several nights before, he had returned immediately to his accommodations, shutting himself away inside, not wanting to see or interact with anyone. The Black Beast had a session in store for him, he knew—and what a session it was, the beast's intensity shredding him to pieces. He had been up all night battling it, a raging war within his head.

He entered the church early the next morning, the magnificent carved doors groaning as he pushed through them. They had been carved in 1471, apparently. So many lives had passed through, just as he was now doing, his foggy mind pondered, each separated by time, united in hope. The overcast skies were dark, clouds hanging heavy, rain imminent, the bleakness of the early day mirroring his mood.

Kneeling on the heavily stuffed hassock, he was grateful for the thick cushioning under his knees. He noted the velour fabric was almost threadbare, a sight he somehow found comforting, the worn patch an indication of the many people before him who had kneeled in this exact spot, praying, and hoping for answers to their own prayers, maybe for their own miracles or maybe for redemption he pondered. His bicep femoris muscles were stinging, given his longstanding crouched position that was unmoving, unrelentingly letting him know of their pain. *I deserve pain*, Alif thought. *At the very least. I need to suffer for my sins. Pain is what keeps me grounded to this life, lets me know I'm alive although I am already dead inside.*

His head bowed, but his eyes looking upward, he watched the elderly woman at the front of the church, her aged body heavily bent over, her testament to a life of hard work. She swung the straw broom in her gnarled hand backward and forward, the bristles connecting with the stone floor, the rhythmic swishing sound almost hypnotic. She stopped momentarily, reaching her palm behind her, rubbing vigorously at the small of her back. Simultaneously, she also tried to straighten up, repositioning her spine to what Alif surmised was a more comfortable angle. Her eyes turned up toward the magnificent stained-glass windows, the early morning sunlight filtering through, the beauty of a new day dawning, the promise of new beginnings, yesterday gone, tomorrow not promised. The sunlight's early rays danced across the glass encapsulating the resplendence, throwing myriad rich colours across the ornate gold altar. The rhythmic swishing of the broom started again. Church had become his place of peace; the tranquillity was soothing, helping marginally to calm his jangled nerves, seeming to help dampen the demons that relentlessly tortured his fractured soul.

Ever since he'd started visiting places of worship whilst living abroad, the denomination irrelevant, he'd found the space calming, providing him an inner sanctum, embracing his tired and battered soul, soothingly so. A place to lay his soul bare, a place to just *be* with no expectations, no requirements. Feeling two lone tears escape each eye, the thin rivulets meandering down his cheeks, he left them to freefall. Ever since the night in the tavern with that woman, her name evading his mind at this precise moment, the dark thoughts he had worked so hard to repress were again solidly etching their way to the forefront of his troubled mind, demanding their own attention. As much as he tried, he could not hold the tears back any longer; the intensity of his emotions was immense. The waves of blackness crashed stormily and with full force into the shores of his mind, cataclysmic in their intensity, showing no mercy. The pain was relentless; he couldn't escape it, no matter how hard he tried, his memories still as raw and ragged now as they had been back then. The prayers he had learned by rote, therapeutic at one stage, comforting, guiding him like a beaming light out of the darkness and despair, like a lighthouse to a ship, were now waning, their effectiveness diminishing. Keeping the demons at bay was a constant daily battle, exhaustingly so. He had come to understand that there was no greater wealth than peace of mind, but it was an elusive wealth to him now. Nothing could give him peace.

His head was heavy in his hands, and he could feel the tears hanging off his chin, clinging before releasing their clutches, dripping onto the floor. His anguished thoughts wandered to the past, his mind easily conjuring up the image of his beautiful and beloved Yasmina, who was always with him, encapsulated, he thought, *in my heart, my mind, my soul. The essence of her looms ethereal before my eyes, seemingly tangible, her aura real. My Yasmina, my darling beloved Yasmina. I can sense her all about me.*

Clutching the pew in front, he could feel the skin stretched taut over his clenched knuckles, his eyes tightly shut. His mind digressed back, sinking into the past; his emotions were anguished, sorrow and frustration roaring through his veins. He could hear his breath, jagged and raspy, the pain interminably overwhelming, an anguished howl uncontrollably emitting from the depths of his broken soul. He tried to claw himself back to the present, to escape the dark hole into which he was hurtling yet again, the second time in as many hours, the hole that the Black Beast pulled him into regularly. He tried to remember the sequence of thought-calming techniques and self-preservation taught to him by Dr. Yassouf, a well-renowned, highly sought-after psychiatrist he'd been seeing, but the techniques failed again. The demon was still too strong for him.

He registered a touch, a hand gently placed on his shoulder and was immediately placated, *her softness, ahhhh my Yasmina is back.* . . . He rested his head on the hand, Yasmina's, caressing it with his cheek, soothingly, comfortingly. *My Yasmina is back. Did she ever leave?* His mind was muddled, its murky depths confused. Suddenly, a sound, distant as if travelling through a tunnel, weaving in and out, infiltrated his emotions, abruptly pulling him back into the present, his beautiful Yasmina instantly disappearing as if chased away, a ghost vanishing once again. He cried out to her, trying to grab her essence, to hold her close, but there was nothing in his grasp except vacant air.

A soft voice registered at his mind's periphery, its murmur intrusive into his thoughts, whispered in hushed tones nearby: 'Are you alright, sir?'

Jolted by the realness of the voice, the hand, Alif realised it was not his Yasmina's touch on his shoulder. He released his breath in one long, slow expulsion, then looked up, blinking, rubbing his eyes. *No, no, no.* He shook his head disbelievingly. *Not that woman again? I can't bear dealing with this vulgar woman again.*

'Are you alright, sir?' The question again, soft. Immediately he was annoyed at the audacity of this woman's intrusion. . . . What was her name? His mind's cogs churned rapidly in recall mode. *Oh, yes, that was it. Elsie.* He was instantly infuriated by her obvious lack of consideration for his privacy, particularly in a place of worship. Somehow it seemed indicative of the same selfishness she'd portrayed the other day down by the beach.

Glaring at her, Alif knew his body language was gruff. 'You again,' he grunted, his voice thick. She stared at him; her eyebrows drawn into a frown as if seeing him for the first time.

'Hello.' Her voice was soft, barely audible. 'I'm Betsy.'

Something about the woman before him—Betsy, apparently— registered in his brain's peripherals. Her mere presence was calming, he realised, but confusion now pervaded his frazzled brain. The gentleness of her tone, her simple gesture of kind words conflicted with the self-centred woman he'd encountered the other day.

'Betsy, not Elsie?' he asked. She paused, fiddling with the buttons down the front of her cardigan, her fingers seeming to twitch nervously.

'Elsie is my sister.' Her statement was simple, but Alif detected a slight hint of disdain. Her hand still rested on his shoulder— it was not Yasmina's as he had believed only moments before, but he didn't push her hand away. He sighed defeatedly, her soothing presence seeming to penetrate his embattled mental armour. Alif's senses were in overdrive. He was quietly intrigued by this woman before him. He realised he didn't want Betsy to move away and so, in slow motion, he slid across in his pew, and patted his hand on the vacated area next to him.

'Sit . . . please.' He looked up at her, knowing how wretched he must look. He registered concern etched across her pretty features.

'You were shaking extraordinarily and rocking backward and forward, sir. I was concerned for you.' Her manner was impeccable. She didn't move from her standing point. The gentle demeanour of the woman before him confused his frazzled mind, his tortured thoughts exhaustingly twisting and turning to the point of discombobulation. Lost for words, drained of energy, he shrugged his shoulders. 'Please accept my apology,' Alif said, his voice breaking

'Tears are the silent language of grief,' she said, the words gentle out of her lips. 'No apology necessary.'

'Sit, please,' he repeated, suddenly realising he welcomed the calming presence of this woman. He wanted her to sit beside him. She remained standing, seemingly unsure, hesitating. *Does one damaged soul gravitate toward another?* His mind threw out the question, *the darkness of pain seeking solace from another damaged soul? Familiarisation of two hurting souls, understanding of one another's pain, finding solace together?* These jumbled thoughts tumbled through his bewildered brain. Where had they come from? It was almost as if a sixth sense had developed within him. He was surprised by the connection or perhaps it was closeness he felt with this woman, for he also sensed a pain within her, a vulnerability.

'I also have cried oceans of tears of late.' Betsy leaned in, her voice barely audible, wringing her hands together. 'They say knowledge is power, but I have come to realise that is not always so. They say ignorance is bliss—now *that* I believe.' Her voice was barely a whisper. She moved slowly, smoothing her hand behind her flowing skirt. He couldn't help but notice its beauty—the vibrant greens, pinks and blues were dazzling with birds perched atop tropical foliage. *It is a happy skirt*, he thought, as she slid into the space next to him.

CHAPTER 17
Alif - Then

Alif sat. Stilled. He had returned home from his time spent abroad in Italy. The act of not moving was therapeutic, the body and soul immersing into one. His mind wandered. The word *act*, referencing being completely still, seemed idiosyncratic. His breathing was slow and measured as he refocused, finding his zone. His lungs ballooned, filling slowly, as he concentrated, counting to eight . . . holding for four . . . exhaling for seven, the eight full, ready to burst. It felt good to have control. The exercise was meditative and soothing, zenning him inward, the immersion restorative, as taught by Dr. Yassouf.

Time ticked by, and he lost track, the crisp chirp of a bulbul nearby drew him in, serenely; its sound was friendly and pretty. He slowly opened his eyes, drinking in the beauty of the lake swanning before him. The lake, nurtured by the elegant gardens framing its perimeter, fanned out graciously in front of his eyes, its tranquillity gently caressing the remaining tension from his soul. The expanse of water evoked a calmness, fanning out from its core, the ripples dancing across the surface, reflecting the blueness of the sky above. He drank in the glory, absorbing the delicious scents of nature. It was the only place he could find any semblance of solace these days, the bountiful peace of isolation offering his fractured mind a minuscule dose of reprieve from the relentless torture of his thoughts.

He eased back, sinking his body deep into the carved contours of Mamma. His mother. His dearly beloved mother. Forever in stone. Quartz granite, the sculpture had perfectly captured her soft lines, her curves, her long hair cascading down her back. After the passing of Mamma, Pappa had commissioned the finest of artisans to create a remembrance garden in her honour. A private garden just for Omar and him, where they could visit, reflect, feel close to Mamma, where they could ultimately and hopefully heal. Resting now, as he leaned into Mamma's stone body, the gazebo shielding him from the intensity of the midday sun, he sat, absorbing the sight before him. Her statue sat at the water's edge, intricately carved, seated on a small wooden platform, the weeping willows elegantly lining the perimeter of the manmade lake, pretty, the longest fronds floating on the water. The sculpture was artistically created, Mother's right arm arched across the back of the seat allowing him to mould his torso into the softly carved lines of her stone body. Its design and purpose were therapeutic, ethereal in her presentation, stationed here for eternity, always waiting, always comforting, always available. So many times, since that fateful day he had sat here, feeling Mamma's presence, talking aloud to her, taking comfort in the solitude.

Omar had laughed at Alif when he'd first heard him speaking to Mamma, his voice talking as if she were right there beside him. 'Silly Alif,' Omar had laughed, always so quick to mock. 'Mamma cannot hear you. You are such a baby sometimes!' He'd said this as he had skimmed stones effortlessly across the top of the lake. Omar wore his newfound defiance like a Kevlar vest, his angry armour donned at Mamma's passing. 'Look,

Alif,' Omar called, his bombastic voice demanding attention. 'Watch how I can skim two rocks simultaneously!' He whooped in delight at his own prowess. His brother's inability to connect to anything on a deeper level other than his own needs these days had never ceased to amaze Alif. Ignoring Omar, Alif had continued to 'talk' to Mamma, having lots to share with her that she had missed out on since her passing. Verbalising his thoughts helped him find clarity and acceptance in his grief. Raya had encouraged his talks with Mamma, saying it was a therapeutic healing tool. He had told her that he didn't use any tools, just his mouth to talk. She had just smiled at that and planted a kiss on the top of his head. She never did explain what tools he needed, but he didn't mind as talking provided enough peace for him in the serenity garden.

'Alif, watch!' The demand was immediate again, interrupting his thoughts. Omar's presence was always so loud and disruptive. Lifting his eyes in the direction of Omar's overtly enthusiastic voice, he froze in disbelief, watching in horror, his line of vision taking on a slow-motion effect. 'I've got you, you vermin,' growled Omar, his lip curled in a sneer, concentration etched hard across his face, his eyebrows a horizontal line, narrowed, so focused was he on his target. He had angled his arm backward as far as he could, before thrusting forward, a torpedo of vigour. The rock left his hand, propelling forward like the missile it had become, hitting the jerboa that was harmlessly drinking at the water's edge, rock and skull connecting, a loud crack, death imminent, instant, blood oozing. 'Bullseye! Perfect shot!' Omar clapped his hands together, and glee spread across his face at his 'accomplishment,' waving his arms in the air victoriously, whooping!

'Why are you always so mean, Omar?' Alif had screamed, disgusted at his brother's obvious delight, his cruelty! 'Ibrahim!'

demanded Omar loudly, ignoring Alif, directing his voice in commanding tones to the gardener who was methodically trimming the hedge near the ornamental wrought-iron side gate. Ibrahim sharply looked up at the call of his name, the hedge precise. 'Come clean up this disgusting mess. We shouldn't be subject to such a sight!' Omar bellowed, the obnoxious authority in his voice impudent.

'You're not the boss of everyone, Omar,' Alif had yelled at him, his twelve-and-a-half-year-old voice croaking and squeaking, breaking with the onset of puberty. So frustrated was he at his brother's constant bombastic behaviour and feeling sorry for Ibrahim having been spoken to in such a disrespectful manner, Alif had tried to assert his independence.

'Oh, yeah!' he yelled back. 'Well, I am the boss of you and the staff, so don't you forget it.' His finger pointed, jabbing into Alif's chest, deflating his stance.

'Boys.' Pappas deep voice had sounded from behind, startling both of them into silence, and they'd turned simultaneously. They hadn't seen Pappa for a week, so busy had his schedule been. Omar ran to Pappa's side, his glee still prominent. If Pappa had heard their raised voices, gruff with one another, he hadn't acknowledged it. 'Pappa, look what I did,' Omar said, pointing proudly to the dead animal. Pappa's eyes followed the direction of Omar's finger; Ibrahim was now scooping the deceased critter into his scoop shovel.

'Good job, son. No place for vermin here,' Pappa had stated, absentmindedly patting Omar's head. Omar's fourteen-year-old brain had interpreted Pappa's words and head pat as approval and he had stood there lapping up Pappa's praise, his grin spreading like a cheshire cat, widely, from ear to ear, his chest puffed out. Omar, his eyes sharp, like shards of glass, had turned toward Alif, daring his brother to contradict Pappa's praise. His inability to differentiate between right and wrong seemed to be getting increasingly blurred, his manipulative and vindictive nature often rewarded by absentee parenting from Pappa.

'Now, come, boys, time for prayer.' Pappa's weary voice dissolved their vision of locked eyes. Turning, Omar and Alif followed Pappa out of Mamma's Garden, falling in step either side of their father. Alif slipped his hand into Pappa's, enjoying his father's gentle squeeze of his palm. They walked united to the mosque as the call for prayer reverberated through the airwaves, the recitation loud and clear, summoning its flocks to worship. Alif had always loved the call to prayer, its sound celestial, invoking the power of belonging, like a security blanket. Forgetting Omar's horrible actions of a few moments before, as the sound drew him into its comfortable embrace, a sereness embodied Alif. The celestial sound pulsated, weaving its power into his soul, infallibly evoking calming emotions of love and tranquillity within him.

His mind was deep in reflection. *So many memories tangled in his conscience, a complicated collection of synapses.* Not for the first time Alif had wondered how different their upbringing would have been if Mamma hadn't of died at an age when both he and Omar were so vulnerable, so very much in need of her. To have had her guiding influence, her presence, always calming and nurturing, understanding of each of their differences.

The tapping sound of approaching footsteps snapped Alif out of his reverie, his meandering recollections reeled back to the present, the tapping, sprightly in its tread. Slowly, Alif raised his head, turning in the direction of the sound, surprised to see Omar approaching, his brother's self-aggrandizing swagger

Traffic of a Lie

perpetuated by his confident step, his sense of self-importance expanding through his chest, pontificating like a rooster defining its dominance. Omar's mere presence oozed confidence. Momentarily, a complimentary thought of acknowledgement flitted through Alif's mind at the sight of his brother. Omar looked classic as always, impeccably dressed in a white linen shirt, a stylish watch adorning his left wrist, chino pants and ultra-sleek navy brogues completing his outfit.

Omar had always appreciated all aspects of fashion, confident in his choices. His dark hair was slicked back with hair gel and glistened under the sunlight. 'Still cuddling up to stone Mamma, I see?' Omar's tone was a mocking sneer. Alif looked up at him. Disappointed. They hadn't seen each other for some time, and this was Omar's greeting. A sigh of disappointment deflated Alif, chagrin at his older brother's immaturity. As if caught in a time warp, Omar's fourteen-year-old condescending mindset was seemingly still obvious when it came to Alif. He chose to deflect his brother's obvious taunt. *Maybe he was like this with everyone?* He didn't know these days.

Leveraging his tall frame into the vacant bench space beside Alif, Omar turned to face his brother, his eyebrows raised as if posing a silent question. 'Are you going to say something, Alif, or remain mute?' There was a haughtiness plastered on his face. Alif pondered his question before responding, 'How would you like me to answer, Omar?' He turned toward him, his voice drained, volleying the onus of his arrogance back onto him. An awkward silence sat between them. It appeared his question had taken Omar off-guard. No arrogant retort flung back at Alif, as was his usual style. Omar slowly moved about in the seat, fidgeting, the vein on his temple pulsing as if with unease. He checked his fingernails, impeccably manicured though they were, before stretching his legs, crossing then uncrossing them before him. 'Like that is it,' he stated, maintaining his insouciance like a veil. Uncertain of what that meant, Alif didn't have the energy for Omar's games or riddles, so stayed silent. Omar, fidgety beside him, flicked a speck of imaginary lint from his pants, smoothing them down before pulling on each of his finger joints, the release of air emitting a loud pop, knowing how much Alif detested the sound, as if baiting him. Alif ignored him, not in the mood for his childish annoyances. *Some things will never change*, he thought with resignation, as his mind returned to his own problems.

'Neither of us has really recovered from Mamma's death, have we?' Omar's words floated across to Alif, interrupting his train of thought, his statement capacious, filling the air between them, taking him by surprise. 'Each time I see you, Alif, which unfortunately is not often enough these days, my mindset seems to automatically regurgitate my behaviour back to that time.' His words released, slowly and deliberately, as if he was searching for his truths, testing the waters of his newfound sentiment. His words of confession hung in the airspace between them, fragile in their temperament. Such a profound statement from his brother piqued his interest, as Alif sat upright, straightening from his slump.

'That got your attention, didn't it?' Omar said, and a quiet, almost self-deprecating laugh escaped his lips. The Omar Alif knew always wore his arrogance like a badge of honour, but he refrained from verbalizing that thought, saying instead, 'Your perceptive words have caught me off guard, Omar. But, yes, I have pondered that question more times than I care to count.'

'I still think of Mamma all the time, you know.' His voice had muted tones, was reflective, as if Alif hadn't spoken, as if he were absorbed in his own headspace. 'I still miss her. It bothers me that with each passing year, I seem to lose a bit more of her . . . her smile, her scent, her voice . . . a bit more of all of her.'

His confession lingered on the air particles between them, its concept abstract. Alif welcomed this new feeling of warmth that was unexpectedly evolving between them, nodding his agreement, understanding exactly what he meant. Alif patted his brother on the shoulder, and he reciprocated. It felt good, this new bonding of solidarity. Alif quietly suspected that Omar's new lady love Helena may have had something to do with this new side of his brother, this side of being more in tune with his feelings. Alif liked it. It was a healthy step forward for Omar, so consumed in anger had he been since Mamma's passing, and in parallel, healthy for the two them, their relationship. They sat and chatted for an interminable length of time, the amicable breeze of words between them fulfilling.

The afternoon rays of the sun began to dip on the horizon, dancing glints of light shards bouncing off the lake's surface. Omar looked at his watch, citing an appointment to get to. In unison, they both rose, Omar pulling Alif into a tight embrace. 'Thank you, Alif. Let's not leave it so long next time.' Omar zealously patted Alif's back. He reciprocated, before Omar departed, then sat back down on Mamma's bench, his spirits slightly lifted.

CHAPTER 18

Sabrina – Then

Mother's voice raged inside Sabrina's head again . . . like a broken record, its spiel almost continual these days. *You can change being fat but you can't change being ugly.* Her mother's caustic words always simmered just beneath the surface of her subconscious, like a pot on the stovetop, almost at boiling point. Mother's vicious tongue, its incessant taunting, was designed to keep Sabrina in her place. The caustic barbed remarks had had maximum impact for as long as Sabrina could remember. She had nursed her mother through her final months, but even on her death bed, Mother's parting words, as she had taken her final gasping breath had been, 'Ugly is as ugly does'—words full of hurt and spite. And for what purpose? She always had to have the last word, was unable to stop herself, and her words were like poisoned darts, without exception striking their target. Sabrina shook her head, trying but failing to eradicate the nasty voice, its constant, insidious taunts . . . each word like a disease, poisonous tentacles . . . forever, firmly spreading through her brain. A voice she could never rid herself of!

Some days were slightly better than others when she did manage to keep Mother's 'voice' at bay, to focus on her routine, mundane as it was, but today was not one of those days. The scorched, parched earth beneath Sabrina's thin soles was burning her feet. She tried to walk as fast as she could, but the going was difficult, particularly with her cumbersome load, both physically and mentally, Mother having a forefront position today. Sabrina hitched the heavy basket into the crook of her right arm, placing her left-hand underneath, helping to support the weight. The basket was filled with her day's baking effort, an array of Malik's favourites. *'Any wonder you're fat'*—Mother's voice referencing her big bake. *'I have to sample my baking,'* she retorted to the nasty bitch. She pushed Mother's presence aside... admittedly... Sabrina thought, Fatima had taught her daughter well. Yasmina's cooking skills were admirable, but of course no one fed her Malik as well as she did.

She reached Malik's house and turned onto the dirt path leading down the side. The wooden fence slats lay broken and fallen across the path in places, the dilapidation resembling an obstacle course. She was suddenly struck by the lack of noise; the silence was deafening. She stopped in her tracks. A sense of unease settled on her as she realised there were no sounds. The banging of pots, taps being turned on and off washing vegetables, footsteps on the linoleum, smells of cooking permeating the air—the sights and sounds that were indicative of the preparations of the evening meal and conducive to this time of the day. Weird? Pausing, she felt a sense of foreboding overcome her. Something felt off, a tingling sensation darting down her spine, something was wrong, very wrong.

With trepidation she continued forward, carefully navigating around the pile of rubbish at the house corner, the pile too large for her to step over. She edged sidewise, her foot catching on the outer spillage of discarded food scraps. A rat darted across her foot, obviously disturbed from its feeding, nearly causing her to lose her balance. Startled, she cursed loudly at the dirty, bloody verminous creature as it scuttled away, hesitating momentarily before she continued forward and entered the lean-to. From this angle she could see Malik seated, hunched over in his chair, his back to her. He was rubbing his hands through his straggly, thinning grey hair. She paused beside the table that was located just inside the doorway, bending down to put her basket on the floor, the table cluttered with debris. The corner of the basket caught on the broken, jagged edge of the table, upending it sideways, the contents spilling out ... probably ruined! *Damn*, momentarily her thoughts were angered as the food tumbled from the basket, food she had spent all day preparing, now damaged, spread across the floor, two of her bowls shattered in the process. Quickly perusing the mess before her, she noted with satisfaction that she should be able to salvage some of the food. Malik still hadn't moved, even with the noise of her entrance. She ventured forward into the kitchen ... slowly, hesitantly, her nerves now feeling rattled. She gasped, her sound loud. She was completely unprepared for the scene before her.

Her breath caught in her throat as she slapped her hand over her mouth, an involuntary jerk reaction to the scene of carnage that lay before her. The horrendous, bloodied mess that met her line of vision was incomprehensible. As if turned to stone, she froze to the spot. Disbelief rattled through her brain as she tried to make sense of the locus that had assaulted her senses, of the scene laid out before her eyes. *The scene that would irrevocably change their lives forever*, she realised. Her nostrils absorbed the stench, its vileness caught in her throat, its intensity ballooning the room, emitting a metallic tang to the airspace. It took her breath away. She tried to suck in air through the palm of her hand, which was firmly squashed against her lips, making it difficult. Silence. The enormity of the situation rendered her immobile, mute, as obviously it had Malik. The large clock on the wall ticked methodically. Finally, she found her voice. 'What... the... hell... have... you... done... this time, Malik?' Her sentence was staccato, disjointed, barely more than a whisper. She could feel her heart palpitating, each beat faster, more intense than the previous beat. Bile rose, burning her oesophagus on its ascent, raging like the cut of a thousand swords up into her throat.

Mother's voice—forever the parasite embedded deep in her brain—opportunistically rose once again to her mind's forefront, sneering gloatingly, ranting inside her head. *Useless daughter, useless offspring.* Sabrina's fists clenched and opened, her anger escalating uncontrollably. *Useless is as useless does,* Mother's parroting voice clawed at the inside of her head, incessant, unrelenting. A gut-wrenching scream pierced her ears, passed from her lips. The sound was primal, and emanated from deep within her, like a wild beast, bellowing deafeningly. Unable to control her anguish, she thrashed her head sideways. No, no, no, no.... 'What the hell have you done this time, Malik?' she repeated, screaming as she turned toward her son, who still hadn't moved from his chair and was sitting there motionless, as if he'd turned to stone.

Mother's screams exploded inside her head, rising to a crescendo, chanting, taunting her like a record player's needle that had become stuck in its rut, over and over and over, *useless is as useless does.* Sabrina raked the side of her head with her fingernails, their long, jagged sharpness tearing down the sides of her face. She could feel the pain of her skin tearing, her fingernails like sharpened talons. She grabbed at her hair, tearing it out in clumps, her desperation acute. Trying, but failing to eradicate Mother's insidious voice from inside her head, her hysteria continued to build. She screamed again, 'What the fucking hell have you done, Malik?' Her anger was explosive, uncontrollable. She lurched at her son, grabbed his arm, digging her nails in deep. She shook him violently, mustering all the strength she could. Her detestation of him was absolute, and it manifested itself in violence. She kicked, punched, and lashed out at him as she looked at the bloodied pulp of a mess lying on the floor . . . that was Yasmina.

Yasmina was slumped in the corner of the room, her head cocked at a sickening angle, unnatural, her mouth gaping open, teeth missing, nose smashed and flattened, her face a bloodied mess of pulp, almost unrecognizable. A large flap of skin hung down partially covering one eye, the blood pooling in her long lashes. She registered the carnage before her, disbelieving. Yasmina's arm was bent in several different locations, a bone protruding from above her right elbow. Her eyes were open, staring, unseeing. Tick, tick, tick. Loud. The clock marched on, measuring time, emphasizing the fragility of time now denied Yasmina. Sabrina stood there momentarily, breathing deeply, trying to process the visual carnage that lay before her. The barbaric brutality of the scene was difficult for her to process. The reality was heartbreaking. Looking over Yasmina's body, she realised that the only part of her that remained intact, not brutalised, or butchered, was her big, swollen belly. She stared, unmoving, frozen to the spot, unsure what to do next, trying to compose her thoughts.

Sabrina saw a very slight movement from within her daughter-in-law's dead body. Very slight. The movement in her swollen belly was like a small wave gently rolling under the skin. Her heart wrenched for the woman that lay before her.

'I'm sorry, Mummy. I did ask her if she wanted a beating.' Malik's voice, taking on a childlike quality, quietly spoken, broke into Sabrina's thoughts. 'She hadn't prepared my evening meal.' Sabrina turned to face him, stunned, muted to the spot, utter disbelief in what she was hearing.

'And did she say, 'Yes, please, Malik, please beat me senseless, until I'm nothing more than a bloodied pulp of a mess?' Her anger exploded at the absolute revulsion she suddenly felt for her son. She hit him across the back of his head with her open hand; the slap was loud, and she hoped it hurt him. Turning back, she looked at the repulsive scene before her, her stomach heaving, roiling on the waves of disgust. Unable to control it, she baulked, the contents of her lunch now spewed over Yasmina's foot, the sight adding insult to injury. She wiped the dripping vomit from her chin with the back of her hand before heaving again, the repulsion emptying the last remnants of her stomach contents, her midday meal, involuntarily for the second time.

'Shut up!' she caterwauled at Malik as he started to say something. A few minutes of silence had passed. At this point she didn't want to hear another word that came out of the useless imbecile's mouth, such was her disgust with him. She couldn't even bring herself to look at him. The air was still around them. Malik rose from his seated position and walked over to the doorway where the basket's spewed contents from that morning's baking spree still lay. Bending down, he retrieved a cookie from the floor and stuffed it in his big gob, crunching noisily like a starving pig. His actions repulsed her.

The strong stench of death was starting to permeate the oxygen around them—*not unlike rotting fruit*, she thought. Realising that time was of the essence, she reached her decision on how to move forward in sorting out this mess Malik had created. She knew what she must now do. *Ugly mind, ugly deeds*, Mother's uninvited voice chipped in, clawing at the back of her mind, Mother always having to say her piece. Ignoring Mother's taunt, Sabrina walked over to the kitchen drawer.

CHAPTER 19

Henrique – Then

Holding his hand up, palm flat, the universal signal to stop, Henrique silently communicated to his three comrades behind him, and each was instantly compliant. Silent. Listening. On directive, they collectively had been assigned a mission to retrieve the woman of the house that they now stood before, their directive to treat this heavily pregnant woman gently and without force, taking her to a safe house where she would be protected. The woman would be unaware of the situation she was about to be faced with, and apprehension and trepidation were expected reactions from her when his team accosted her unexpectedly—such was their brief. They were to reiterate to her that she was safe with them, to pacify her fears, not to worry, to enlighten her with the code word Alif and she would understand—or such was the expectation. If she was still resistive, chloroform was the plan, to render her unconscious for easy removal with minimal noise or distraction, eliminating creating a scene and arousing suspicion should her husband be nearby.

Information had been forwarded in their brief that the husband should still be out in the fields at this time of day, a smooth, easy assignment. Henrique, a special operations commandant, was well trained in emergency, terrorism, and threat situations, having served numerous tours of duty; the men assigned him were collectively and individually in their own right highly skilled. The mission had appeared obscure from the divulgence, not their normal realm of operations. The directive had been issued from the higher echelons of government with few details available. Even with the scant details forwarded less than two days ago, it was obvious he and his team were doing someone else's dirty work. It was not really their jurisdiction, but after many years in the job he was aware of the politics of the hierarchy they worked under, knowing fully that both he and his men dare not refuse or question an order from the ranks above. The ramifications for insolence were draconian, retribution harsh.

He fanned his arms in a half-circular motion, pointing. Chad and Ayoub deployed silently to the front of the house, the recipients reading his hand-communicated directives. But something seemed off. The scene before them was devoid of sound or movement, the silence deafening, unusual for this time of day. Suddenly, Henrique sighted movement, a woman, hunched over a bulky basket she was carrying, manoeuvring her solid frame surprisingly deftly, scurrying out the back door. She had paused, looking slyly left and right before continuing cautiously, trepidation obvious in her movements. From his hidden position, Henrique noted her facial features. Her look was maniacal, her scowl making her look unhinged, dishevelled. Her cheeks looked flushed, as if great exertion had been applied. Her apron appeared wet—or was it bloodied? It was hard to tell from his vantage point whether the colour was brown or crimson. This was not the woman they were after; of that he was 100 per cent certain. She was too old by all accounts to begin with according to the description he had been issued, but she was definitely a vital part of this operation—of that he was without doubt. He moved forward stealthily; the older woman's back was now in his sight as she turned down the side of the house, shifting the basket to her other arm. Following, he gained ground on her cumbersome form.

Deafeningly, seconds apart, without warning, two loud gunshots spliced the silence. Instinctively, both he and his comrade Jorge dropped to the ground, invisibilising their bulks. It was a survival tactic for when no hiding protection was available, a manoeuvre they'd performed often in combat in the vastness of the unrelenting desert settings. More gunfire rained out in their direction. An ambush. An anguished split-second cry reached his ears, his eyes darting sideways to take in Jorge, situated several metres to his right. He noted Jorges's limp form on the ground, a gaping wound annihilating his head. He felt momentarily saddened but knowing that detachment was important in field operations, he averted his attention back to the task at present. His senses were on full alert. He looked up and realised he'd lost sight of the older woman. Chancing it, on all fours he scrambled to the corner of the house, his knees protesting with pain. He righted himself to a vertical position when it was safe to do so as he reached the back perimeter of the house. With his back against the wall, he inched sideways in the direction of the woman who had exited only moments prior. Reaching the farther corner of the house, he cautiously looked around the side and was unfortunately not surprised to see Chad and Ayoub's lifeless forms on the ground. Their head wounds were testament to their demise—they'd been the recipients of the initial two gunshots he'd heard. Crouching low, he kept his back against the house wall, taking stock of the situation, and was again struck by the unnerving silence.

Momentarily, he reflected on his previous mission, which had featured the same overwhelming silence. Now in retrospect, he knew it was the calm before the onslaught. The enemy was plotting, the element of surprise decisively shifting the balance of power with minimal input. The enemy's manoeuvre had been successful in its administration, disarming his platoon, taking them all by surprise. The impact had been deadly and maximum. Knowing that now was not the time to dwell on that past failure, Henrique shook his head, ridding it of the uninvited thoughts, a habitual action when he was trying to clear his line of thinking. With his thoughts returned to his current situation, he tried to take stock of the unenviable set of circumstances in which he now found himself. Three dead men, an unsighted shooter, an older woman mysteriously scurrying from the scene and a yet-still-unsighted younger pregnant woman who was the subject of the mission.

Standing upright, keeping his back against the wall, he stealthily and slowly backtracked along the wall in the direction he'd come, reaching the dilapidated lean-to that was clumsily attached to the back of the house. Elongating himself along the side of the doorway, with a swift stance, his body held rigid, gun poised outright, he rapidly twisted left, right, left, his eyes darting, taking in every detail he could, quickly and effectively. He surveyed the inside of the room by the back door. Ascertaining that no one was present, he cautiously proceeded, first entering the small kitchenette, stepping forward from his doorway position. He was taken off guard by an unmistakable cloying stench, metallic and violent, his nostrils flaring as they took in the full force of the assault. It was a stench he recognised only too well from his time in combat, a stench he'd inhaled more times than he cared to remember. He knew, without any doubt, that he was inhaling the unmistakable stench of death.

The area was silent. The silence of the dead. Cautiously moving to his left, slowly and inaudibly, he edged along the outer perimeter of the room, past the aged agar, its surface filled with pots, old and dented, all exhibiting a bubbled effect created from years of use. He also noticed that although old, each pot was scrupulously scrubbed clean. Was this by the caring hands of a woman who took pride in her home or by the flustered hands of a woman filled with fear of her husband's wrath? He wondered. From the sight now before him, he knew the answer.

He sighted her leg first, poking out from beyond the kitchen table in the middle of the room. Her leg was bent at an unnatural angle, an angle that only a broken bone would allow. He moved around to the end of the table, his line of vision following along up her body. He was unprepared for the barbaric sight before him. He gasped loudly, the carnage before him akin to a slaughterhouse. The sight sickened him to his core, was offensive to the eyes.

'Holy Lord, Jesus Christ,' he cursed loudly. His voice ragged, his cheeks puffed in and out deeply as he tried to control his breathing and the rising bile in his throat. Realizing his errant words as a man of God, he admonished himself immediately. The Lord's name should never be used as a profanity. But unfortunately, it was what had come instantly to his mind at this particular moment. He heard his voice; it sounded distant and hoarse, choked with emotion and the frustration at the futility of it all.

Without hesitation he lowered his tall frame to kneel by the girl's head. Immediately he knew this must be Yasmina, their mission, their subject. 'Yasmina.' His voice was anguished as he looked at the young woman lying before him, barely out of childhood. Slowly, he leaned over her and gently took her hand into his. His big palm dwarfed her dainty little hand as he enveloped it, his fingers performing a patting motion as if to pacify her—a pointless action, he knew. He felt suddenly overwrought with emotion, the scene before him triggering a memory of another scene, which he'd faced two years before after his platoon had been ambushed. Innocent young lives had been obliterated within minutes, mercilessly, murderously. That had been his last assignment. He'd been relegated to desk duties after a year off work, recovering from post-traumatic stress disorder. There's only so much horrific carnage the human mind can absorb before it says *enough is enough*. The memories flooded his head. The grisly details. The lack of respect for the living. The feeling of hopelessness that these young lives must have felt when they had met their insufferable endings, when it had been his duty to save them. His emotions were once again filled with anguish. This assignment was meant to be a simple and easy one for his return to field work.

He turned his attention back to Yasmina. 'I am so incredibly sorry. We were too late. We were supposed to save you.' He whispered quietly to her even though he knew she couldn't hear him. He could hear the huskiness of emotion in his voice. Yasmina's head was lying at a right angle against the wall it had been smashed against. Carnage surrounded her in the most abhorrent of circumstances. He looked into her deep brown eyes, the window to a person's soul, which once would have been so full of life and vitality but were now callously dulled by the brutality of death. She lay staring, unseeingly, directly ahead, the terror of her final moments evidenced with the dark pain etched deeply in her face. The mutilated scene before him was incomprehensible. Gently, he ran his hand down her face, closing her eyes, careful not to pull on the flap of skin overhanging her right eye.

'Rest in peace, beautiful Yasmina.' He deemed a prayer appropriate in the circumstances. He reached over and took both her bloodied hands into his, hands he noted with which she had evidently fought in vain to defend herself. He bowed his head in respect. 'Lord Jesus, holy and compassionate,' he began, inhaling thickly with a deep breath, then continuing, 'Forgive Yasmina's sins. By dying, you unlocked the gates of those who believe in you. Do not let this beautiful young soul . . .' The words rolled slowly off his tongue, ragged with emotion. He paused again to compose himself, wanting to do justice to this young lady as her soul departed this earth, onward bound toward her heavenly journey. The futility of the brutality before him caught in his throat once again, and his voice choked with raw emotion. His weary mind stalled, heavy with sentiment.

He tried to stabilise his ragged breath, concentrating on breathing in deeply, out deeply, struggling against himself. Barely able to contain the intensity of his emotions, he propelled forward, continuing, wanting to do Yasmina justice. . . . 'Be parted from you, but . . . by your glorious power give her light, joy, peace in heaven where you live and reign forever.'

He sat there. Pausing. In silence. Then, uncontrollably, without his conscious permission, errant tears begin to escape his eyes, snaking down over the stubble of his face, one after another until they were one continual leak. Like rapids bouldering down a stream, over the imperfections of scars on his face, dripping off the edge of his chin. His tears landed on Yasmina, blending with her blood. 'I'll get the animal who did this to you,' he vowed.

Pulling himself together, Henrique heaved himself off the floor from his crouched position, clarity confirmed, and with that clarity, the cognizance of his next move. But, first, even though he knew full well that he'd be compromising the procedure of a crime scene, he hunted about the house for a blanket or something equivalent to cover the mutilated and exposed abdomen of the girl before him, to afford her a modicum of dignity. Her womb gaped open, horrifically hacked and shredded, her body's innards protruding where her unborn child had resided only a short while before. The jagged, serrated edged knife was discarded ruthlessly next to Yasmina's lifeless form. He felt the glimmer of an idea taking form at the back of his mind, the idea taking definition. He knew without a doubt what he had to do next.

CHAPTER 20

Malik – Then

'Ma,' Malik sang out from the back of the house, puffing heavily after having run across the barren paddock from his own house. He'd swung the door open energetically; the splintered wood of the doorframe had caught the thread of his shirt, inevitably ripping yet another ragged hole in it. There was no answer from Ma. He knew she hadn't wanted to speak to him back at the house, but she'd had time to settle down now, he'd decided. 'Bloody door,' he cursed, as he wrenched his hooked shirt off the nail that it was caught on. *Another fix-it job I haven't done*, he muttered, thumping the doorframe heavily as he passed through it, a small dot of blood appearing on his arm. It seemed the nail had caught his skin as well as the fabric. The unfixed door would be another berating from Ma. He was expected to attend to all the maintenance of this shithole of a place as well as his own. *He couldn't be bothered maintaining either.* 'Ma . . . I shot 'em all . . . dead!' he'd called loudly. Ma would be proud of him, of that he was certain, but as usual he also knew that she wouldn't verbally acknowledge any accomplishment he'd achieved.

Walking into the kitchen, he saw Ma leaning over the old straw basket she'd dumped on the end of the table. Her head was turned sideways, words hissed out of her mouth like a serpent about to strike, savage. 'Shut up, just fuckin' shut up,' she said in a shrill voice. She was talking to Grannie again. *Jeez.* Rolling his eyes, Malik thought, *Grannie had been dead, bloody dead as a doornail for years, but Ma still talked to her, or more accurately argued and cursed at her continuously. She looked like a madwoman most of the time talking to thin air.*

'Ma, did you hear me? I shot 'em all dead, outsmarted 'em, I did.' He raised his voice this time so she would hear, so proud was he! This had been his moment of glory, gaining an advantage over those vermin that thought they could sneak up on his property, his home. He'd showed 'em! His raised voice seemed to have the intended outcome, catching Ma's attention, her wrinkled old, wizened body suddenly acknowledging him as she looked up from the basket she had been so focused over.

'You blubbering idiot.' Her wrinkled face, hardened by years of sun damage, turned from cursing Grannie toward his direction. 'Now we'll be targets, someone will be after us, mark my words . . . always such a completely useless dumbass, that's what you are! Do you think you can go about shooting people like that, shooting 'em dead without repercussions?' she screamed at him, anger spitting out her gob, a big globule of chunky spittle landing on the side of his neck. Disgusted, he wiped it away with the back of his hand, her lack of appreciation for anything he did infuriating him. She was nothing more than an unappreciative bitch! He stood there clenching his closed fists, visualizing smashing one into her ugly face, but trying his hardest to refrain from doing so. That would give him so much satisfaction, he thought, a wide grin spreading across his face.

A meek cry emitted from within the basket, the sound pitiful, diverting both their attention. 'Shit, Ma, what you gonna do now?' The vision of Ma slicing open Yasmina's abdomen, without hesitation or seemingly showing any sign of remorse, was still fresh in his mind. The blood and guts that had horrifically spooled out, as she had wrenched the baby from its safe space where Yasmina had grown and nurtured it for nine months, had been barbaric. The repulsive images had been scrolling across his mind manically as if they were on a continual reel since Ma had committed the unimaginable. He didn't mind a bit of blood and guts—shit, you get used to it growing up on the land, slaughtering your own animals and all, but holy fucking Christ that had been next level demonic! Ma had turned manic; her frenzied actions had been deranged.

Yeah, sure, he'd hit Yasmina around, slapped her up a bit, made sure she knew what her role was in his household. After all, he was her husband, it was his rightful duty to make sure she knew her place, to teach and guide her and all that. A man had to do what a man had to do; otherwise, how else would his woman learn her place in his home, learn how best to serve him? But Ma's actions . . . holy mother of Satan! That was another whole level! The enormity of the situation had been surreal; the egregious act committed by Ma was beyond imagination, unfathomably abhorrent. He paused, impressed with his use of words. He had heard Yasmina use some big words and had committed them to memory, even though he'd pretended to ignore her most of the time. It made him sound educated. He smiled, pleased with himself.

He turned his attention back to Ma. Not for the first time recently, he looked questioningly at the woman before him, his mother. He noticed an acrid body odour emanating from her person. She looked unkempt, dishevelled. Her dark eyes were wide, darting about, looking manic as she cursed the imaginary grannie standing next to her. Her fat, dirty finger was shoved into the baby's mouth, placating the tiny infant, if just for the moment.

His confusion of the situation suddenly transcended into one of clarity, the clarity of insanity standing before him—his mother's insanity, which he now realised had been unravelling for a long while. 'Stupid bitch, she's as mad as a hatter,' he said, seeing it all so clearly now. He stared at her with complete disgust, digesting the situation they now found themselves in, trying to think quickly—*what to do next?* His Ma was singing to the baby. The poor baby was trying to push Ma's big, fat, dirty finger out of its mouth.

Without warning. Click. He felt it, he heard it. The unmistakable cold, hard metal of a Glock registered unsuspectingly against the back of his head, the barrel pressure forcible, uncomfortable. 'Don't move, fuckwit.' The low, menacing tone hissed in his ear. He hadn't heard anyone enter, so focused had he been on his deranged mother before him and the infant. *This isn't good*, he thought. Averting his eyes, not daring to move his body whilst he tried to work out his next move, he looked across at Ma. The mad bitch was completely unaware of a fourth person having entered the room. Her brittle and hard voice was grating— another imaginary argument with Grannie in full swing! Jesus, what a bloody circus, he thought. *What must gun-wielding man think?* If it weren't so serious, the scene before him could almost be comical! Almost!

'Hands behind your back, arsehole.' The deep hiss came from behind him, threatening in tone, his situation odious. Malik knew he was done for. When there's a gun pointed at your head, options are limited other than to comply. He felt the cool metal of the handcuffs engage one then both of his wrists, deftly and swiftly performed. He heard the click, securing his hands, rendering him ineffective. The element of surprise was always the most effective tactic to bring down the enemy. His mind was racing as he tried to formulate a plan, but he knew time was against him. Without warning, pain exploded across his temple, shards of white light pierced his eyeballs, the brutal force of the gun creating maximum effect, smashing into his skull. Ma's ugly face turned toward him. It was the last thing he saw before the floor leapt up to greet him, blackness enveloping.

CHAPTER 21

Adeline – Now

The muffled broadcast announced that flight KT169 would commence boarding in fifteen minutes at Gate Fifty-One. After a six-hour delay the information was welcomed, evident from the waiting passengers' reactions, reiterated by their cheers, claps and 'about time' exultations. Frustrations that had boiled over earlier, a result of the constant delay announcements, were now replaced with joy.

Leaning over to retrieve her bag from the seat beneath her, Adeline felt a whoosh of air pass by her head. An exuberant red-headed boy executed a cartwheel, all gangly legs and flailing arms, complete with a jubilant vocabulary, seemingly pleased with both his athletic prowess and the flight boarding information. Cheers nearby from his siblings erupted. 'Tommy, stop it.' His mother's harried voice reprimanded her energetic son. 'You nearly kicked that poor lady in the head!' She looked apologetically in Adeline's direction.

'No harm done,' Adeline responded silently praying she wouldn't be seated anywhere near the woman and her five rambunctious children during the long flight ahead.

She needed peace and quiet, her mind craved solitude. She wished she could wrap her mind in cottonwool to cushion the battering it had received after reading Mother's letter. She had cried—oh . . . how . . . she'd . . . cried. Buckets and buckets of tears, partnered with anger, anguish, uncertainty, myriad emotions hitting her with such ferocity, totally unprepared had she been for the turmoil from Mother's unexpected passing and her subsequent revelations.

Six weeks earlier, her life had been orderly, stable, recognizable. How could one's life and everything she'd ever known change in its entirety and complexity in such a short space of time? 'Humph, peace and quiet, what a joke,' she sniggered with contempt, a loud snort escaping her lips. The man standing in line alongside her darted a quizzical sideways stare in her direction. 'Oops, did I say that out loud?' she mused.

'Good afternoon,' the flight attendant, her voice pleasantly accented and melodious, greeted her as she scanned the bar code on her phone, the beep indicating she was authorised to proceed through to the boarding gate. Moving forward, Adeline proceeded through to the plane's boarding corridor, grateful to be advancing at long last. The flight attendant stationed at the vessel's entrance greeted her, politely, impeccably attired. *She looks stunning,* Adeline admired. The attendant's smiling eyes genuinely matched the radiant smile on her red lips, lighting up her entire face with warmth and joy. Her demeanour was most welcoming.

Adeline reached her seat easily, given that she was at the front section of the plane in row 3A, and stowed her luggage in the overhead locker compartment and her handbag into the console adjoining her seat. She settled herself in efficiently, buckling up, ready for take-off. The cabin was a hubbub of excited voices, the din of humans massed together in a contained space palpable. Chatting and 'excuse me's' filled the airspace as people tried to pass each other in the narrow walkways as they found their allocated seats and stowed their luggage in the overhead lockers. The cabin staff was prepared for take-off and, a short time after the preliminaries and safety measures were effectively actioned, the plane finally took to the skies.

Two hours later, feigning sleep, Adeline closed her eyes. Georgina and Ruby's incessant natter beside her was draining her already frazzled state of mind. *Why do people consider it necessary to divulge their holiday plans, travel reasons, and anything else that popped into their head to a complete stranger when seating themselves on a flight?* Adeline wondered. Shrieks and laughter ensued as the two women alongside her clinked their glasses, regaling the 'victory' trip on which they were embarking, retracing their European vacation adventures completed some fifty years earlier. The trip was a celebratory victory of surviving the hardships life had apparently thrown at both of them. As the two women animatedly conversed, Adeline smiled and nodded politely, hoping she did so in the appropriate tête-à-tête gaps, her mind only partially listening to the women's conversation. Preferring that they would leave her out of their confabulations altogether, she diverted her attention to the multitude of jumbled thoughts that were currently bounding through her head, trying to process them into some semblance of order.

Her eyes flew open at the sound of Tommy's sudden shriek, its pitch registering gratingly on her brain. She was unaware of how long she'd been asleep. His shriek also interrupted Georgina and Ruby's reminiscing about a man they'd met in Greece in 1974, wondering where he was now. Adeline twisted her body to look behind her to see what all the commotion was about. She saw the boy Tommy, seated ten rows behind her, his indignant shrieks of 'Getting girl germs!' were loud. 'Mum . . . Matilda . . . drank . . . from . . . my . . . can. Her . . . mouth . . . touched . . . my . . . can, MUM.' Oblivious to the disruption he was creating, several other children added their voices to the ruckus, canting their innocence at Tommy's accusations.

Adeline heard the mother's tone, firm but placating: 'Tommy, Billy, Tilly, each of you take a deep breath and reflect on your behaviour.' Adeline marvelled at the woman's calmness. *Truly, did this reflection, deep-breathing stuff work on overwrought kids?* she couldn't help but wonder; however, she was not left wondering for long before the bellow of 'MUM!' as Tommy's wails of despair escalated. Seemingly not, she decided. Not wishing to stare, the mother not needing prying eyes to make her feel any more uncomfortable than she perhaps already did, Adeline turned forward again, Ruby's eyes twinkling at her. She must have missed something Ruby had said. Obviously trying to diffuse the situation, the flight attendant could be heard offering Tommy a fresh can of a cool drink, Adeline noticed. Satisfactorily, it seemed to appease the boy with the catastrophe averted as it now appeared all was well in Tommy's world as peace and quiet was restored. At this point she couldn't help but wonder why she hadn't taken that temazepam tablet Penelope had offered her at the airport prior to leaving. She would have welcomed oblivion at this stage.

By the time the flight entered its third hour, the passengers were satiated with meals and drinks, and a sense of calm permeated the cabin as the passengers start to settle in for the long haul ahead. The curtain that divided first class and economy lapsed open where the flight attendant's trolley had caught its edge. Peering backward again into the cabin behind her, Adeline saw Tommy. The boy had his headphones on and was smiling broadly at the screen before him. He seemed enraptured with what he was watching, she noted, with crumbs cascading down the front of his shirt, remnants from his recent snack undoubtedly enjoyed it seemed. Shaking her long hair out of its updo that she'd carefully crafted that morning, she placed her eye mask on, positioning the soft elastic behind her head before allowing her weary body to sink comfortably into the contour of her seat. Her mind was an elixir of excitement and nerves, all mingled together, like a tightly wound clock. Simultaneously wonderment and trepidation also filled her at what awaited at her destination, which was now only hours away. There was no turning back now.

CHAPTER 22

Adeline – Now

The thrum of the engine was silenced, a flick of a switch from the captain, the aircraft finally stationary on the tarmac, their destination reached. Adeline peered excitedly out of her cabin window, the butterflies in her stomach intense, the anticipation of what lay ahead manifesting her enthusiasm. The flight had been smooth and uneventful, the passengers eventually settling easily into their in-flight routines; even the children on board had been contented and quiet. She had fortunately welcomed sleep for several hours, a deep and peaceful sleep that had taken her by surprise and she had awakened feeling relatively refreshed.

An hour before their estimated time of arrival, the captain's deep, smooth voice had permeated the aircraft's sound system, explaining first in Arabic and then in English that, due to a technical error, the aircraft was unable to connect to the terminal walkway and alternatively they would be disembarking from the tarmac. The passengers' reactions had been nonplussed, being that they didn't have a choice either way. After the captain's announcement Adeline had proceeded to the bathroom, changed her clothes, re-applied her make-up, and coiffed her hair: a welcome refresh.

Standing to collect her belongings, Georgina and Ruby had wished her well with her onward journey, their excitement obvious. Likewise, she had reciprocated their kind words, bidding them safe onward travels, a genuine warmth radiating from their smiles as they all shook hands. Watching them, she silently berated herself regarding her earlier uncharitable thoughts about them. After all, they were only being friendly, including her in their conversation, she internalised. Not for the first time of late, she was disappointed in her presumptuous judgment of other people and her lack of tolerance. Her current state of mind these days was constantly overshadowing her normal character, a fact of which she wasn't proud. The flight attendant opened the cabin door, her beautiful persona welcoming them all to their destination. She thanked them for travelling with the airline, and said she hoped to see them again soon. Stepping out onto the mobile stair platform outside the aircraft's door, Adeline was blindsided by the intensity of the heat that bombarded them.

She left the intense tarmac heat behind, and the blast of cool air as the automatic doors parted was a welcome relief upon entering the airport terminal. The heat was next level, even compared to Australian mid-summer temperatures, she thought. Sweat meandered down the back of her neck, creating ringlet tendrils through the loose hairs that had escaped her top knot bun, which she had so carefully arranged only an hour before. The bustling terminal was a smorgasbord of people, a plethora of differing itineraries, each determining their convergence at this point in time. The air was eclectic, the buzz of people, such a diverse range of nationalities, everybody on a mission, a destination to reach. She had always enjoyed airports. The atmosphere was one of excitement, of new destinations, new adventures or returning to loved ones. She couldn't help but get caught up in the excitement of it all.

However, on this journey, she was also on a purposeful mission and knew she must keep moving. She exited customs, where the system was still of the old character, requiring lining up and being visually sighted and the passport manually stamped. She was then escorted by an airport staff member, sailing through the collections hall's sea of unfamiliar faces into a nearby lounge. She scanned the signs being held up and saw the digital frame bearing her name. Excited for a glimpse of familiarity the sign evoked, she waved enthusiastically whilst eagerly edging her way forward.

'Hello, hello!' she called, waving her hands about, before stopping in front of the frame holder. She offered her hand in greeting. 'I'm Adeline, so pleased to meet you.' The frame holder, smartly dressed in a dark suit and cap, propped his digital frame effortlessly under his arm and took her hand, his grip firm, before politely relieving her of her bag she had slung over her shoulder. His genuine smile lit up his face, emanating from his eyes. 'Welcome, I am pleased to meet you,' he enthused, his accent thick. A true gentleman, he bowed his head graciously toward her, his English stilted. 'My name Sharif. Come follow,' he beckoned, heading to the right and boarding the downward escalator.

Following immediately, not wishing to lose sight of the only person she was marginally acquainted with in this foreign country, she quickened her step. Sharif, whilst short in stature, was nimble and light on his feet and was already some distance ahead. Disembarking the escalator, they entered what she assumed must be a private parking bay and saw a sleek black

Rolls-Royce parked ahead of them, the only car in sight. Her sandal heels clacked rhythmically with each step as they connected on the polished concrete floors as she walked across to the car; Sharif's footsteps were silent in his shining leather loafers.

Opening the car's trunk with the click of his key fob prior to reaching the vehicle, Sharif effortlessly swung her luggage into its cavernous depth in one swift movement before opening the car door for her.

'Thank you, Sharif.' She nodded her appreciation before gratefully sinking her body into the interior, its black leather upholstery luxurious. Sharif gestured toward the middle of the vehicle and her eyes followed his outheld hand. Reaching across the console, she appreciatively retrieved the cold, damp hand cloth attractively arranged on a silver tray. The corner of the silken cloth was ornately embroidered with the same emblem on the flag located on the front of the car she had noticed when embarking. Located next to the cloth were two gold embossed tubes—one hand cream and one sanitiser, their titles in both Arabic and English. She applied the delicately fragranced hand cream followed by the sanitiser, and her hands instantly absorbed the moisture and were left feeling soft and beautifully fragranced. An iced mint tea and biscuit were precisely placed alongside the cloth on a separate tray, another welcoming touch as she realised how parched and hungry she was suddenly feeling. She dabbed the wet cloth on her brow and the back of her neck, its coolness a welcome relief against her hot skin. She sipped the tea and found its freshness reviving.

Sharif eased the car out into the bright heat of the day; its engine purred like a contented kitten. Despite starting to feel a bit weary, given that she'd only slept a handful of hours in the past thirty, she felt adrenaline pump through her veins. Not wanting to miss the passing landscape, she peered through the darkened windowpane and absorbed the passing sights. Ping . . . the high pitch of her phone signalled Penelope's presence, thousands of kilometres away, her distance seemingly of another dimension at this point. Yet another message was coming through . . . the umpteenth since Adeline had landed, the fifth since she'd entered the car, she registered.

She saw Sharif's eyebrows rise questioningly in the rearview mirror, directed at her. 'My sister,' Adeline offered by way of explanation. Sharif, tilting his head slightly, shrugged. 'You no want talk to sister?' His question was a statement; his eyebrows rose again, looking like they were about to disappear off his forehead.

'Actually, no, Sharif, not at the moment . . . I don't,' she answered. She noted the weariness in her own voice, as Sharif evidently did also, one eyebrow rising considerably higher than the other, then both synchronising, knitting together decisively, before he looked away. Concentration was etched on his face as he negotiated the tight turn ahead, easily controlling the bulky vehicle they were seated in. A comical thought crossed her mind, and a giggle escaped her lips: *man, this guy doesn't need to communicate through spoken language*, she couldn't help but think—*his eyebrows communicated adequately . . . taking on a lifeform all their own!*

Her thoughts reverted to her pinging phone as she reached over and put it on silent. Without even checking she knew it was Penelope; her whiny voice from their last conversation was still fresh in her mind. 'Addy, Addy'—her childhood pet name for her, which had followed into adulthood—'please, please, please!' Her whining pitch rose with each *please*. 'Let me come with you! I can support you with whatever.' She'd flapped her hand dismissively in the air as if Adeline's current problems were little more than an inconvenience, to be batted away. 'And heaven knows I desperately need a holiday with everything that has been happening.' With lips pouting, her head tilted downward, her eyes had bored into Adeline, as she pulled her woebegone forlorn look, which admittedly had always worked on her in the past.

As much as she dearly loved her sister... after reading Mother's letter Adeline knew that this was a journey she needed to take on her own. She didn't have the temerity to be accommodating Penelope's self-centred behaviour, her anxieties or her complexities. For the first time in her life, it was time for Adeline to put herself and her needs first and foremost. Mother's letter had shaken her to her very core. Suddenly learning that her entire life had been based on a lie, a lie in which she had had no say, had been devastating, to say the least. Innocence was the price she had paid for her mother's deception. On reflection, she thought, there had been inklings. But she'd never questioned her different looks, her dark hair, olive skin. She knew that she and Penelope had different fathers, but now she also knew that they had different mothers. They were not biologically related at all. Horror filtered through her as the recollection threw itself in her face again. That knowledge had shaken her to her very core... the first of many bombshells that she soon learned were about to assault her. She'd tiptoed through the letter as if she were negotiating a landmine, scared of what was going to hit her next, to disarm and disfigure her life as she had known it.

The revelation that she was the product of a completely different existence to her entire family had hurt Adeline enormously. She'd felt like her identity had been completely erased, the shock she'd felt akin to an electrifying jolt. The physical pain in her heart was real. *Who am I, why, how?* So many questions had clouded her mind incessantly over these past few weeks. How had Mother kept the enormity of her secret locked away in her own heart for so long? What sort of twisted person did that? No matter from what angle she tried to look at the situation she couldn't condone her mother's actions. After the initial shock and rereading Mother's letter many times over, her reaction had turned to anger. Anger at the lies, at the deception, at being denied the very basic of knowledge that was her right to know. It had consumed her, her loathing had escalated wildly ... and ... so purely by association she had decided she wasn't going to include Penelope on her trip ... her mother's daughter!

Without realizing it, Adeline had been holding her breath, so consumed had she been in her thoughts, a massive sigh escaping her lips. Looking up, she saw raised eyebrows in the rearview mirror ... Sharif's kind eyes directed at her. His eyebrows asked if she was OK. Smiling, she assured him she was OK before diverting her attention to the passing scenery outside her rear seat window. The car engine purred quietly, and the comfort of the vehicle was soothing as they gently slowed to a halt, the red traffic lights ahead dictating so. Peering out of her window, she was appreciative of the normality of the scene before her. She noted the shisha bar located on the street corner opposite them. It was filled with men, congregating in their groups, relaxed, chatting, their smiling faces conversant together. They were friends catching up, she surmised, discussing the normalities of their lives, their jobs, children, hobbies and such. She found the scene comforting, the normalcy warming. The patrons turned their attention toward the Rolls-Royce, which was stationary a short distance from them. Some of the men stood and bowed, some bowed their heads from their seated positions, a display of respect.

Traffic of a Lie

Sharif gently urged the car forward as the traffic lights changed to green. She couldn't help but wonder why the city bothered with traffic lights, such was the chaos of the vehicles on the road. Road rules seemed non-existent, with horns honking, people traversing the eight lanes of traffic, navigating their perilous paths, hands held out front identifying their intention to cross. Their vehicle became stationary again, traffic congestion making it impossible to move. Sharif's patience was admirable; he was nonplussed by the chaos around him—*used to it, I guess?* she thought. A giggle escaped her as she looked across at a corner souvenir shop, noting the oversized, enormous novelty ladies' knickers strung across the front. For what purpose, she didn't know, but she thought of her friend Andy in Australia, always playfully making fun of his partner's knickers . . . a joke amongst friends. She was tempted to take a photo and send it to Andy but before she had chance to do so they were mobile again.

The drive was interesting, the city eclectic, a cacophony of extremes, at odds with itself, poverty and wealth coexisting, traffic chaotic, the tapestry of the local people's lives so interwoven in all this chaos. Slowly, they inched along, and it wasn't long before they left the noisy, chaotic metropolis behind them, with the landscape giving way to farming land. It was primarily olive trees. The plantings were vast, miles upon miles, all symmetrical, row upon row. The regimented structure of the groves was impressive in their entirety, a complete juxtaposition to the chaos of the city only moments prior.

She felt connected to this orderly structure, which was decisive, systematic, methodical—the exact fabric of her being. She identified with the landscape before her. Déjà-vu? She couldn't explain. This shift in her equilibrium took her off-guard. She was unable to clarify her feelings. *It was almost as if she belonged there.* She could feel the turmoil of the past few weeks ever so slightly dissipating, unravelling its twisted tentacles, which had been gripping her heart with an intensity, a heaviness . . . now waning. A warmth was slowly infiltrating her veins, warming her being, a thawing. A moment of great revelation . . . sudden in its presence . . . an epiphany struck her. She was where she was meant to be at this exact moment in time, she realised. Comfortable in the lap of serenity, secure within herself. Feeling as if the dark clouds that had been burdening her every thought over these past few weeks had suddenly dissipated, bursting their seams. She relished this new emotion, this tender sentiment of peace. The car purred to a gentle halt, the magnificent wrought iron gates slowly opening before them, welcoming them to enter. The beautiful tree-lined driveway snaked its way before them as they proceeded.

CHAPTER 23

Adeline – Now

Sitting on the ornately carved marble seat, the stone arms of her paternal grandmother encompassing her, Adeline felt relaxed and at ease. The cool marble was smooth and glossy, its shiny exterior luxurious, the very essence of it creating a soothing and calming ambience. The breathtaking beauty of the scenery that fanned out before them evoked a sense of serenity. The lake, equally calming and energising simultaneously, lapped and rippled with the slight evening breeze. The sister's watched in admiration as a bevy of swans came into view, gliding across the lake's surface their elegant movements both graceful and flowing, emanating a regal quality. Adeline's gaze peeled over the lilies, deliciously exotic, their large green leaves floating effortlessly on the water, adorned by myriad flowers—reds, pinks, oranges, lavenders and yellows, all harmonizing together, like a rainbow, blending and complementing each other in unison whilst also individualistic. Serenity.

'Princess Adeline.' Penelope drew in a deep breath as she uttered the words. Seated together, the two girls held hands, an easy silence between the sisters as they drank in the calmness before them.

To say the past six weeks had been tumultuous for the both of them would be an understatement. Revelation after revelation, the story . . . her story, their stories. Infinitely separate, but completely joined. Several weeks after reading Mother's letter, Adeline had invited Penelope to join her. *She was her sister, after all*, she had internalised, as far as she was concerned, on all accounts—apart from biologically, as it had turned out. Penelope was just as much an innocent victim in the deception that had been their childhood. Adeline could feel a slight shift in her spirit, the impetus of her existence now unfurling like a leaf opening to the sun, the dark, thunderous events of the past weeks starting to take a slight step backward, this new dawning a rebirth. She had embraced the offering, the truth, piece by piece, as it was divulged, softly portioned to her incrementally, with the greatest of consideration and respect to her by her father, Prince Alif. He was a father she hadn't known existed until a few weeks before. Eminently gentle in his guidance, he told her story, allowing her the space and time to digest her history in all its beauty and ugliness. His patience and empathy were unconditionally loving and kind.

At her insistence, he had left no stone unturned. Adeline wanted—needed—to hear every detail. She had hung onto his every word as he had explained his great love for her mother, Yasmina. He told her how Yasmina had been a poor peasant girl, how they'd met by accident one day in her family's barn at the back of their property, how, although not rich in a physical sense, she was abundantly rich in the love of her family. Yasmina had been beautiful and clever, her personality and presence vivacious, with a profound thirst for knowledge. She had the intelligence to achieve so much but was unequivocally disadvantaged by the patriarchal society into which she was born. Papa had spoken lovingly of their secret meetings and trysts, of their conversations, laughter, and of falling in love, his eyes misting over as he digressed to that time. But their time together had been cut brutally short when it was announced that Yasmina was to be married to another man. Papa had been bereft at his own pusillanimous character, disgusted by the promises he had made to Yasmina, unintentionally misleading her in the belief that he would come for her, that they would be wed and then never following through with his promise due to her having been betrothed to another man. He'd rebuked himself every day since, and his torment was still obviously palpable. It had eaten at his soul, knowing as he did of the intense pain his absence would have caused his beloved Yasmina.

As a result, he had never married. Yasmina had been his one true love and, after losing her, he had deemed himself undeserving, unfit to experience the joy of happiness again. He was of a gutless and unworthy character. He had held himself accountable. He had sunk into a deep depression. He'd battled his demons, 'the black beast', for many years. He'd been so overwrought with despair he had eventually decided to confide in his brother, Omar, to ask his perspective on the situation. Surprisingly, Omar had been supportive and accommodating, genuinely listening, not passing judgment or being his usual arrogant self. Omar had said to let him think about it, to see if he could come up with a solution. Omar had then left the country on a business trip. Some months later Alif had decided to visit Yasmina's parents himself. It hadn't been a decision he'd made lightly, knowing that she was now a married woman and unsure of the reception he would receive from them. But he needed to absolve his desertion of her and take ownership of his actions, take the chance in trying to right his wrong, regardless of the repercussions. He loved her with all his heart and the twelve-month interim period since he had last seen his beloved Yasmina had only strengthened his love and confirmed his commitment. He wasn't proud of his behaviour but throughout the entire twelve months, his conscience had chipped away incessantly at his lack of integrity, his soul yearning.

He had decided he would explain the whole story to her parents, sure of himself in the belief that they would understand his reasons and support him in his quest to marry their daughter. How wrong he had been. They had listened to him without interruption, afforded him the courtesy to explain. But after he had told them his story, it only seemed to fuel the flames. Her parents had been consumed with grief, absorbed in their own torturous pain at the recent passing of their beloved Yasmina five months prior. Needing to make sense of their daughter's heinous murder, they had blamed him, Alif. Contempt had been etched across their faces, accusingly stating that if he had been a man of honour and integrity, if he had of followed through with his promise to come back for Yasmina, to marry her, she would still be here alive today. He had agreed with every word her parents had flung at him. This news coupled with the asseveration that Yasmina had been with child at the time of her death had utterly devastated him.

Pausing, Pappa had taken a long, drawn-in breath. The pain of his words was evident in the depth of his expression. Continuing, he had explained how he had left the farm that day, gutted beyond belief by the news of his beloved Yasmina's horrendous demise. He had only found out some years later that his brother Omar had sent in a team with the intention of rescuing Yasmina and subsequently bringing her to the palace to be reunited with Alif. This information had been a surprising revelation, a most unexpected and noble gesture from Omar.

The devastation of hearing that the rescue plan hadn't been successful had been difficult to digest. His beloved Yasmina had been brutally beaten by her savage and violent husband, Malik, then butchered at the hands of her demented mother-in-law. Henrique, the only survivor of the mission, had gone rogue, opportunistic with greed taking over when he realised the baby was of royal blood, the news delivered to him by Malik's mother, Sabrina, as she had lain dying. Seizing the baby girl after killing Malik and Sabrina, he had sold her on the black market, his aristocratic English friend whom he'd met years earlier when serving as an undercover agent having the right connections and had received an admirable sum. It had set Henrique up comfortably for life. Henrique had immigrated to Australia and assumed a new identity, wanting to be inconspicuous. He'd studied accounting and built a new life for himself. Erasing the man he had once been, he had reinvented himself as Edward Wharton. Liking the sound of an English name, he had worked hard on acquiring an English accent. Adeline and Penelope had physically baulked at the mention of Edward's name. Yet another revelation to comprehend, so overwhelmed with shock and horror had they been at the atrocities of the man they had always looked up to and respected. The compounding of yet another deception burdened the girls throughout their childhood. Just like a long and complicated jigsaw puzzle, they were slowly starting to connect the pieces, one by one, each of them slotting in together as the timeline proceeded.

Pappa, pausing, had patted Adeline and Penelope each on the knee at their obvious shock of hearing Edward's name. He continued, explaining how he, Alif, had been totally bereft and devoid of functioning and had ventured to Italy on a soul-searching sabbatical. Thoughts of suicide had been constantly at the forefront of his mind, the darkness of his deep, black depression demonic and torturing. There, he had met twins Elsie and Betsy, who were identical in looks, but polar opposites in character. Elsie was egotistical, bold, brash and self-centred, whilst her sister Betsy was outwardly warm, with an embracing and gentle nature by comparison. But, as he was to find out, Betsy was fighting her own demons. He would often see her in the local church, praying, searching for her own answers, some form of divine intervention. He had felt a kindred spirit in Betsy, her outward gentle demeanour in contrast to her deep turmoil and anguish.

One day he and Betsy had been the only occupants in the tiny church. In hushed tones, they'd started conversing. Unburdening her heavy heart, Betsy had detailed how she'd recently inadvertently overheard a heated conversation between her parents, details of their business, the source of the wealth and luxury that she and Elsie had been brought up in and were accustomed to. Her parents operated a baby-selling racket, conducted on a global level, the dirty logistics cleverly disguised under an adoption business framework. She, Betsy, had been descending the opulent staircase of their three-storey London residence, heading out to the art gallery where she was working part-time, art being her passion and focus. Her parents' raised voices had caught her attention, the heat in their aggressive words being flung at each other atypical in relation to their normal placid tones. The argument had been about the lucrative sale of a bastard princess. Disbelieving what she was hearing, she had dropped her handbag, the contents clattering loudly against the mahogany balustrade as they free-fell. Her parents, alerted to her presence instantly, had stopped their harsh words mid-sentence and strode out to the lobby, horrified at the realisation of the content of the conversation their daughter must have overheard. Not wishing to verbalise their abhorrence, their demeanour geared into instant overdrive, one of damage control; her mother's speech had been rapid as she tripped over her words trying to exonerate the reality of the vileness of their 'business' actions with excuses and implausible claims, the reasons fanciful.

Elsie and Betsy's trip to Italy was designed to remove the girls from the home environment, to palliate the depression that had overcome Betsy from the knowledge she now carried around like a leaden weight of her parents' dirty business practices. Elsie had delighted in the trip, thought the holiday a fabulous idea, a celebration of graduating college, no expenses spared, everything they wanted at their whim, oblivious to the real reason behind their Italian adventure. Betsy knew it was a pay-off from her parents in the hope that she would forget the knowledge with which she was now burdened, knowledge she could never forget—nor could she forgive the callousness of her parents' greed, their brutality of ripping families apart whilst keeping their hands clean.

Betsy had been warned not to breathe a word of it to anyone. The repercussions would be harsh for her parents and, by association, her and Elsie. Upon hearing Alif's story, the revelation of his royal status—a prince, at that—his love of Yasmina, their intimate times spent together in the barn, her rushed marriage and the sale of a bastard princess, Alif and Yasmina realised that the timeline aligned. They deemed the facts too coincidental to be overlooked. Betsy had verbalised her secret to Alif, the tortured soul before her, even though she had had strict directives from her parents to never tell anyone. It had filled her with a sense of relief to unload the heavy burden of the despicable knowledge she'd been carrying around, the crushing knowledge that had been weighing her down. Between them, Betsy and Alif had hatched a plan to try and locate the stolen princess.

Elsie had misconstrued the newly formed closeness between Alif and Betsy as a relationship. Her jealous, manipulative nature had erupted. She'd been green with envy, wanting and determined to have Alif for herself, maddened at his blatant rebuttals of her advances. One night she had come across Alif and Betsy on a clifftop. She had hung back, ensuring she was obscured from sight as she observed the two of them, deep in conversation, their body language amicable, at ease with each other. Elsie's hackles were raised as she witnessed a familial hug between the two of them before Alif turned away, leaving Betsy with an endearing smile, blowing her a kiss. Seething, Elsie had bombarded her sister, rage and jealousy consuming her, lashing out, shoving her sister hard. 'Traitor!' Elsie had screamed, spitting the word out with such venom the ferocity of her sister's attack had taken Betsy by surprise. Betsy had spun around to face Elsie, the element of surprise causing her to lose her footing. Betsy had grabbed frantically, her hands waving manically trying to seize hold of the poorly maintained guard rail that ran along the clifftop, but to no avail, her eyes wild with realisation that there was nothing to stop her freefalling. Elsie had stood there, frozen to the spot, smirking momentarily, watching her sister, as she began to fall, plunging headfirst into the cavernous dark depths of the cliff rocks below, killing her instantly.

Alif had only been a short distance away and upon hearing Elsie's raised voice, he had turned and watched, absolute horror etched on his face, witnessing Betsy freefalling over the cliff, as if in slow motion, the image now forever etched in his mind. Knowing full well that she couldn't possibly have survived such a fall, he had bounded as fast as he could down the rocky cliff wall toward the floor below.

Pappa paused, his eyes deep with obvious sadness as his mind reverted to that time, that place again. His pause spanned several minutes before he had slowly continued the story, his voice barely a whisper. Elsie, sighting Alif, had fled from the scene, mad, blind panic overtaking sensibility. An enquiry of sorts had ensued, the local Italian constabulary insouciant in professionalism and knowledge. Their negligence and amateur investigation had been a disastrous fiasco. The findings of their enquiry had inevitably ruled Betsy's death accidental. Alif knew different. He had left Italy immediately, putting as much distance as possible between himself and Elsie. Another woman he cared about was now lost because of him.

Upon his return home, his thoughts were consumed with the knowledge that possibly he had a child out there somewhere. But in a world inhabited by over six billion people, locating his baby would be like trying to find a needle in a haystack.

Pappa's voice faded away, and the three of them sat in silence. Adeline and Penelope gently squeezed one another's hands, both lost deep in their own thoughts. The pieces of the puzzle were nearing completion, the whole picture presenting in its completeness. Both hugged Pappa.

CHAPTER 24

Mother's letter

'My dear darling Adeline.' Tears sprang involuntarily to her eyes, always deep and rich. Baritone, Mother's voice rose from the page she was holding. The nervous tension she had felt over these past weeks was now pulsating by way of a headache, jackhammering at her temple. It was now one week since the reading of the will. Deciding she had procrastinated long enough, Adeline was now sitting in her study, cosy, with the open fire crackling, a cup of tea at the ready, the liquid strong and black, determined to read Mother's letter today. A storm of magnitude raged outside, hissing and snarling with unseasonal intensity, remnants from the cyclone that had rampaged the Kimberly region over the past few days, now weaving its trail of destruction down through Central Australia and into South Australia. The wind howled as it whipped around the corner of the house, its tentacles filtering under the pool blanket, the bubbled polyethylene thwacking up and down against its watery contents beneath. Finally... putting procrastination to the side, she began.

'The fact that you're reading this letter means that I have passed.' Mother's words came at her directly.

'I have languished exponentially over the years, the urgency escalating since my cancer diagnosis, on how to explain the facts to you, Adeline. Where to even begin? Oh, how I've languished... written a million letters, or so it seems... only to scrunch them all up furiously, ball after ball, into the wastepaper basket... frustratingly so.' Adeline heard the hesitancy in her mother's writing, obvious, heavy, a BUT looming.... 'The truth is ugly, very, very ugly, my darling daughter, and I am indelibly ashamed in my part in this whole sorry mess! Believe me, my dearest Adeline, I am penitent. My guilt-ridden conscience is unrepentant, haunting. It's constant call—plaintive, insidious, incessant, over the years, clawing at my skull, at my dulled moral sense.'

Pausing, the heaviness of Mother's words before her chilling, the slight tremor in her hands escalating to a shaking movement, the words jumping about before her, Adeline placed the scrawled cursive of her letter on the oak wooden desk in front of her, leaning over it to read, a feeling of dread encompassing her. Mother's baritone voice continued: 'I tried to talk to you face to face... so many times... tried to take responsibility for my actions... but I couldn't bear the inevitable look in your eyes, your judgment, your disgust, your disappointment and the hurt that I knew without an element of doubt would be staring back at me through those big, soulful brown eyes of yours. Knowing that, I have opted to take the coward's exit and put pen to paper. I have not been honest with you, Adeline, and I am incredibly ashamed to say so.

'As day follows night, inevitably I knew this time would come, but a part of me didn't want to acknowledge it, for to do so would highlight my true character and inevitably change both your and Penelope's perceptions of me. Deservedly so, I guess? My two little girls who had always looked up to me, their mother, with such admiration and unconditional love. A pure love that I surely didn't deserve, but one that I devoured whole and completely. I didn't want to ever tamper with that love. So, I said nothing. Who knows? Maybe it's a predisposed genetic embellishment of my parentage or maybe I truly am rotten to the core? I have pondered this question my whole adult life. Was I born a substandard, pathetic human being or am I a product of my environment? The age-old question, hey? Nature or nurture? This question has tortured my mind.' Adeline paused, absorbing Mother's confession, thinking that she was rambling, as if she was delaying what the letter was really about.

'Back to the facts. . . . From the moment I first laid eyes on you, nursing your little body in my arms, my love was instant and intense. From the tip of your perfect little nose, so beautifully defined, complementing your dark eyes and impossibly long eyelashes, to the tips of your perfect little toes. You were the perfect baby, easy, reaching your milestones effortlessly, growing into a gentle, caring and considerate child and then the strong, independent woman you have become. I am unequivocally proud of your strength of character and integrity, attributes at which I failed miserably . . . I know that.'

She sensed a hesitancy emanating from Mother's stalled ramblings, and a queasy feeling began to rumble through her stomach. She stared at the letter before her, the feeling of foreboding breaking out in prickly goosebumps all over her arms . . . the foreboding of a big fat BUT looming on the precipice.

'There is no easy way to say this, Adeline . . .' The air around her pulsated with tension. . . . 'The truth is you are not my biological child. I did not give birth to you, nor did your father die as a decorated soldier shot down in his fighter jet in a war over the Middle East. Both lies. Deception, it seems, has always been my go-to, my forte. I'm so sorry, my beautiful girl. I've misled you enormously, a deception you didn't deserve. The lies, so much easier for me to digest, are a selfish parallel of the truth I'd convinced myself to believe in, easier than accepting the cold, hard facts of the ACTUAL truth. I've stalled enough though. . . . brace yourself, sweetheart.' Adeline paused again. Mother's words were chilling, and a shiver spiralled down her spine. She drew in her breath deeply, her body shuddering, her heightened senses on alert, scared of the content to come. 'You were the victim of a brutal kidnapping.'

A thunderous clap hammered overhead, making Adeline jump. The howls of the storm raged outside, its intensity swirling, dark and thunderous, as if in unison with Mother's own thunderbolt admission. The sharp jolt felt like a nail being driven into the coffin of her frazzled head, lightning splintering the night sky. Her eyes peeled out the window, drawn by the brightness, the row of tall conifer trees on the other side of her study window taking on a ghoulish outline in the staccato bursts of lightning.

She reread the last sentence in disbelief. Perhaps she had misconstrued the words? Blinking, she focused back on the page. The same word still blurted before her eyes. *Kidnapping*. The word was nonsensical to her overloaded brain, and an insidious numbness slowly wove its way through her veins, the enormity of her mother's words unfolding before her, alien, foreign, too hard to digest. Her jaw was clenched, tight, holding in the threads of grief and disbelief tangled in her head. As if a dam had burst, a guttural sound spewed forth. She felt it rising, like bile, deep from within her depths, its sound, primitive in its anguish as it thrashed throughout the room. Her mind momentarily disassociated with incomprehension. *Kidnapping*. The word lifted from the page, again and again, throwing itself in her face, horror sludging through her blood, its putrid veracity offensive in its vulgarity. A pill of disgust lodged in her throat, gagging her, its bitterness unpalatable, choking her airway. Kidnapping. *Who am I then? What, where, why?* The questions rampaged, racing, one after another through her head. Another crash of thunder boomed overhead, its intensity rattling the windowpanes, releasing heavy globules of raindrops, each noisily crashing down on everything in its path, unified with the tears of disbelief now streaking down her cheeks. Gulping long and deep, her mind obscured with confusion and disbelief, she endeavoured to stabilise her raging thoughts. She reached for some tissues, her hand beneath the desk, opening the drawer, her eyes not wavering from the words before her. She wiped her leaking eyes and blew her nose.

She paused and was still for a long while, a detached paralysis settling within her, a vagueness swirling through her mind that now parallelled the word *mother*, a word that had always evoked emotions of love and tenderness, but now signalled confusion and disbelief. She focused inward, trying to regulate her ragged breath. She felt the need to try and calm herself, to initiate a state of reactive detachment, before she was swallowed whole by this consuming monster of grief that was unravelling before her. Knowing that there was more to come, with a trembling heart, she read on.

'Edward was an SOS in the king's army. He and a small team were sent to rescue your mother, Yasmina, a peasant girl who had been forced into a consanguineous marriage. Yasmina was also pregnant with you at the time, but pregnant from a liaison with Crown Prince Alif... your father. The men were ambushed in their mission, with three of them losing their lives, an older woman taking off with you (I will spare you the barbaric details of how that came about), her imbecile son, Yasmina's husband, Malik, trailing her. Edward, who was known as Henrique at the time, was a highly skilled marksman and the only survivor of the ambush, had tailed them, tracking to the old woman's house. Killing the woman and son, Henrique seized you in the basket, discarding the directives of the operation, seizing an opportunity to embellish his own coffers.

'He had contacts in London . . . within the black market, baby adoptions, knowing he would fetch a grand price for a princess. Horridly to say, these London contacts were my parents. My identical twin sister Betsy overheard them arguing one dreadful night about the sale of a baby—a baby princess. She was disgusted by the details she'd overheard, the gravity of the knowledge weighing heavily on her moral compass. We were sent to Italy for a holiday . . . supposedly to help Betsy forget what she had overheard. This is where we met Alif, a chance encounter. Serendipity, maybe? His grief and Betsy's knowledge, conversations had, they started to puzzle the pieces together, the facts far too coincidental to be random.

'I had spotted them one night on a clifftop, heads bowed, whispering closely together. Jealousy overwhelmed me, for I had wanted Alif to myself—I always got what I wanted. But. Not. This. Time. Alif had rebutted my advances at every opportunity, preferring Betsy. I was furious. I'd overheard their conversation that night, about you, about being Alif's daughter. I approached the clifftop, coming from behind Betsy, the element of surprise. I snapped, lashing nasty words at her, intentional, each filled with poison, barbed and destructive. I grabbed her arm, my fingers clenched tight and restrictive, so consumed with fury was I that she had lynched Alif away from me! She turned, startled, trying to wrench her arm from my grip. That moment of time has forever been branded into my skull . . . like a hot iron. . . . Betsy's look of absolute sheer terror at the realisation, as she lost her footing trying to free herself from my vice-like grip, gravity pulling her over the side of the cliff as I let go. She plunged to her death. . . . It was devastating . . . happening all in the blink of an eye. But . . . at the same time, also kind of satisfying. . . .

'I had Alif to myself now, or so I thought.'

Adeline's mind chugged to a grinding halt, every instinct in her body recoiling at the scourge of Mother's words, the abstract horror unfolding before her in this trainwreck of a story, incomprehensible. Large, heavy balls of ice, hailstones, started outside, plunging from the heavens, hitting the iron-clad roof above her like a spray of bullets. *Breathe, Adeline, breathe*, she told herself, an all-engulfing terror smothering her airflow, all this ugliness suffocating her. She sat there panting, the minutes ticking by until she managed to marginally regulate her ragged breath, before forcing her attention forward . . . continuing on. . . .

'Despairingly, Alif disappeared after that. I returned to England.' Mother's voice came up off the page once again. 'Once back home, I demanded from Mummy and Daddy that I wanted a princess baby, thinking that if I couldn't have Alif, I would have the next best thing . . . his daughter, or else I would disclose their secret—a secret they were willing to protect at all costs! Threatening, yes. As I said before, I was used to getting my own way!'

Brutal shock and horror roared from Adeline's depths, like a prodded lion, too much information to contain within. Her bloodcurdling screams ricocheted around the room, bouncing off the four walls, assaulting her ears, unified with the thunderous boom after boom, the raging storm outside, now inside. Her screams, primal, filled with anguish, tore at her vocal cords like a serrated knife, the sound gushing forth from her lungs. She was unable to stop. Mother's words hurtled at her, brutal and disgusting. Adeline's stomach curdled with revulsion. Feeling as if she had a front-row seat in a horror movie, a saturation of shock flooded her brain, brimming over its edges, unable to absorb anymore. Stars pirouetted before her eyes, the shards of dizzying sparkles disorientating, the sponge of her brain sodden with information overload. Just when she thought it couldn't get any worse, the shock of what she was reading became almost too much to bear. Her mind was haggard, her head was pounding. Who the hell was this person, the writer, a stranger to her? She didn't even recognise the writer ... the woman she had always thought of as her mother. The realisation: her mother was a psychopath.

Standing upright, Adeline's movements were jaggedly spastic, her action spiralling the chair she had been sitting on, carousing it backward, the carved wooden backrest toppling, gouging a fist-sized hole into the exquisite custom-made mahogany entertainment unit behind it. The two forcefully connected, and the rectangular stained-glass door splintered into a thousand pieces. Adeline looked at the mess, unseeing, the carnage mirroring her state of mind. Trying to regulate her rapid breathing, hyperventilating, she could feel her heart racing, beating so hard she was certain it was going to explode through her chest. She cupped her hands together over her lips. Breathing in and out, in and out, deeply, and slowly, regulating her rapid breath, its rate slowly lessening, she calmed herself and braced for the next onslaught of The Letter. She read on.

'Only problem was that you had already been sold. Henrique's services were hired. Your new parents were reluctant to give you up, but with Henrique's persuasive tactics and Mummy and Daddy's money, they relented. I got what I wanted once again. Henrique, alias Edward Wharton, became our accountant, confidante, protector, as we all relocated to Australia, creating a new life. By this time, I wanted to try and amend my wrongs. I underwent therapy, years of it: severe narcissistic personality disorder, histrionic and borderline personality disorder were my diagnoses—a triple whammy! These titles are not an excuse for my behaviours but go a little way toward helping me understand why I did what I did, why I behaved the way I did.

'My parents had disowned me at this point, disgusted in the person I had become. I'd always thought that was the pot calling the kettle black—they weren't exactly angels themselves.' She could hear Mother's sneering voice referencing her parents. She and Penelope had never met their grandparents, Mother always saying that, as far as she was concerned, they were dead, her voice dripping with sarcasm at every mention. They'd always assumed they literally had passed. *Perhaps not*, Adeline now pondered, instantly deciding that even if they were alive, she had no interest in initiating contact, armed with this new knowledge. The letter continued: 'Meeting Penelope's father Everett a few years later was a ray of sunshine on the dismal blip of a radar that was my life. We were madly in love but that too was short-lived, his leaving me . . . my punishment, I suppose, for my previous sins, but out of it all our beautiful Penelope, our miracle baby, brought new joy to our lives and completed our family.'

Adeline paused again, regurgitating this new onslaught of miserable information. She rubbed the back of her neck trying to massage the knots out of it, straightening her back from its stooped sitting position. She reached for her teacup; not surprisingly, its contents were now cold, but she drank it regardless, the insipid taste insulting as it bumped down her throat. She pressed the gold-edged scalloped rim against her lips. She looked at it with admiration; the cup was one of her favourites. Her mind wandered, grateful for the diversion. She and Mother had collected teacups. Oh, what a collection they had. They considered themselves tea connoisseurs, two amateurs having fun. Her mind conjured up recollections of the wonderful conversations they'd enjoyed over their cups of tea, pausing, before feeling a sketch of a smile crinkling at the corners of her mouth, dimpling at her cheeks. Feel-good vibes began to creep in, slight in their appearance as they filtered through her, weird because nothing felt good now, she grouched. Her mind's gearstick needily journeyed into reverse, as though caught in a time machine, its wheels carousing through to happier times . . . times enjoyed together over her and Mother's shared hobby. The many wonderful hours of conversations discussing all things tea rushed at her, so many beautiful memories. . . .

She stepped on the brakes of her thoughts, pausing, reflecting. Their last tea celebration had only been twelve weeks prior, just before Mother's diagnosis. It seemed like both yesterday and a lifetime ago now combined into one . . . a strange concept. Both of them had been seated at the beautiful wooden table setting positioned in the middle of the rose garden. The table was exquisitely hand-crafted by Edward himself, its wood sourced locally from a magnificent red gum that had collapsed at the back of their property, depleted, the tree a victim of drought. They had laughed and regaled in stories about her recent trip, enthusiastically agreeing on a delectable raspberry tea blend she had picked up in Thailand, purchased from a wonderful family-owned tea plantation located high in the mountainous region of Chiang Mai, where Adeline had recently had the honour to spend time. The thought faded, stripping her from her momentarily mini happy vibe plateau, the memory an age ago now, relegated to history. It had been their fun thing they did together . . . but now her thoughts were tangled, the joy tarnished with heartache. A deep sadness transcended over her, like the final curtain descending after an enjoyable performance, pulling her thoughts forward again into the focus of *now*.

A strange calmness anaesthetised her body, eerily soaking through her. Perhaps information overload? 'What do you think, Ted?' she turned, her ragged voice directed at her plush toy, Panda Bear, sitting in his high-back chair in the corner of the room. Ted had been gifted her on her first birthday. He had been her confidante, companion, and sounding board ever since she could remember. Childhood problems, business decisions, boyfriend calamities—Ted had helped her through it all. 'I know, I understand, Ted,' she acknowledged, talking out loud, his black button eyes staring at her. 'This situation is different than any other we've ever discussed, bigger than any other, isn't it?' Her head swirled as she tried to take stock of the situation. 'I need to find a rational viewpoint of explanation, Ted, apply some common sense to these barbaric words laid out before me. I feel as if I'm reading the words of a total stranger, not Mother, not the mother I've always loved and trusted unconditionally.' Her words rolled out in a semblance of order, like they always did when she confided in Ted. 'This woman on paper, so cruel, so heartless. Remember we watched that film, Ted?' Her mind suddenly clutched at the whisper of a memory. 'That's it,' she rubs at her temples. She massaged the pinpricks of tension now needling up from her neck, wrapping around her forehead. 'It was Easter, about five years ago. A late Easter. Penelope had gone on a school trip to Greece. . . . It was only Mother and me at home.' The memory was morphing clearly now. 'The weather was dreadful—actually, not unlike it is now,' she said.

'Thundery, storms, so cold and wet. Remember, Ted? Mother and I had a movie marathon session. Pizzas and platters, and naughtily an overload of chocolate.' She recalled the stomach ache she'd had the next day. One of the movies had stuck in her mind. *The Three Faces of Eve*. About Eve White, but there was also another personality, Eve Black, who wasn't as nice. But they were of the same person. Eve Black had committed the despicable act of strangling her daughter, but Eve White had no recollection of the act.

'Ted,' she said, her voice a squeak as the epiphany hit her like a slap in the face. 'Do you think Mother has such an illness?' Her thoughts were tangled as she churned this over, a spidery web of hurt and confusion, struggling to comprehend. The complexity of a coexistence of two personalities within the one mind and their ability to commit unforgivable deeds of deceit, without the other identity recognizing them, was beyond her current comprehension. A pang of hopelessness skewered through her heart as she rose, walking over to Ted and picking him up. She wrapped her arms around him, hugging him close, burying her face in the shoulder of his soft fur, grateful for his familial comfort. She sat back down at the desk, placing Ted in her lap, continuing Mother's letter, glad she'd nearly reached the end of it.

'This is my story, Adeline, in all its ugliness, laid out bare for you to digest.' Mother's words levitate through the airwaves once again, rising above the din of the storm. 'I understand that I have no entitlement to ask anything of you at this point, but I do so deeply hope from the bottom of my heart that you can somehow, someday, find it in your heart to forgive me.' Her breath caught in her throat; she was physically baulking at the audacity of Mother's words! She stared at the loops of writing, cursive and elegant, before her, each stroke delivering this story of madness. *How could she even be so assumptive to have written asking for words of forgiveness, after everything she had just upended on her?* Adeline gagged with disgust. Forgiveness was not something she could even contemplate at this minute.

Jumping, her mind was again snapped back to the *now*, startled, as another deafening thunderclap boomed overhead, the vibrations of its intensity sounding as if it was sitting directly on the roof. 'I can't remember a storm of this ferocity for a long, long while,' Adeline lamented to Ted; the malevolent temperament of it somehow seemed in sync with Mother's letter. 'Is it wrong of me to feel this way, Ted?' she asked, a broken anguish of desperation in her voice. A fresh batch of tears rivered down her cheeks as a despondency weighed in on her, leaving her feeling deserted and alone. She reached for another tissue, drawing the box from within the drawer underneath and placing it on the desk, a more practical position. Yearning, she wished Mother were there, and that they could discuss her letter over a cup of tea, work it all out as if it was all just a fictional storyline maybe, something Mother was trying out, or a misunderstanding… to gauge her reaction, her input. She chewed this over in her mind. Confusion took over, clarifying like muddy water that she didn't want Mother there; the mother she thought she had had never existed. Ted's eyes, piercing in their directness, scrutinised her, as a melancholic tension settled once again onto her shoulders, this realisation devastating.

Her phone pinged, diverting her attention, Penelope's name popping up on the screen. She glanced at her name, a shudder tremoring through her at the thought of her biological connection to Mother. The thought scared her about what that could mean for them both, moving forward. Unexpectedly a thread of gratitude slipped into her fibre, taking her by surprise; somehow, as if she'd dodged a bullet, she felt grateful that she had no biological connection to all this vile repugnance. It was as if this knowledge distanced her from the rancid offensiveness of the realities that were scrawled across the pages in front of her. A blend of guilt panged her heart. 'Is it unfair of me, Ted,' she asked, her voice confused. She squeezed Ted tight against her chest, '... to label Penelope in the same box as Mother?'

For all her sisterly annoyances, she *did* love Pen Pen, and her statement settled as a questioning doubt of unsurety in her mind. Kissing Ted on his worn ear, which was threadbare from years of stroking against her cheek, she said, 'Don't I, Ted?' The feeling of Ted against her was the only foundation of support she was feeling at that moment. 'This shouldn't change our relationship, or does it?' Treacly thick thoughts of doubt now clouded her judgment, and she felt doubt regarding everything at this moment, which robbed her confidence. She had more questions than answers.

She sat, pondering, the ornate mahogany clock on the wall loudly ticking away the minutes. Summoning her last ounce of courage, she drew in a deep breath, calling on all her reserves, as if running a marathon, the final sprint of energy needed to get her over the line. Slowly, her eyes closed, she focused inward, trying to stabilise herself. She released her breath, long and drawn out, blowing it against the back of Ted's head, fluffing his fur. Gazing back at the letter, she willed her mind the strength to continue onward, a wave of trepidation washing through her, wishing, and hoping it would all end soon. Mother's voice intercepted again.

'With reference to my will ... to explain ... everything going to Penelope. I needed to make sure she was looked after, Adeline. I hope you understand my reasoning because, as a princess, given your royal parentage, I know your financial needs will be fully accommodated.

'Reading back over this letter, I can only imagine the overwhelming shock, disbelief and probable horror you are feeling in processing it all. Please know, my darling Adeline, that, regardless of how we came to be as a family, my love for both of my girls was real, cemented and totally unconditional.

'I realise I don't have any right to ask anything of you, Adeline, but, please, I beg you, look after your sister Penelope. My greatest fear is the genetic makeup she shares with me.

'All my love forever.

'Your mother, Elsie xxx'

Adeline sat there, mute, immobile, at one with Ted, the information contained in the letter too overwhelmingly colossal to process. Her heart felt like it was in a vice-like grip, a grip so tight it was fragmenting her being.

Her tears dropped heavily onto Mother's kisses, obliterating them all.

CHAPTER 25

Six Months Later – Adeline – Now

To learn that the whole fabric of one's existence had been woven into the cloth of one big, deceitful, fat lie had been devastating, but like the phoenix rising from the ashes, there is always a choice on how to move forward, the choice of rebirth. King Omar, Adeline's uncle . . . a smile escaped her lips at this warming thought—she was still getting her head around this whole new family she'd inherited, a family that had welcomed and embraced her unconditionally with such warmth and love, without hesitation . . . had passed away suddenly, a heart attack apparently, automatically promoting Pappa in the line of ascension to the role of king. Two weeks of mourning had followed, followed by the inauguration of King Alif. Omar was blessed with two beautiful daughters himself; however, the order of succession dictated a male sovereign must be the ruling monarch.

Sitting outside in her own personal courtyard located directly off her palace suites, the trickling waterfall hypnotic and tranquil, Adeline turned her face toward the morning sunshine, its silvery rays awakening to the new day, the golden shards dancing across the waterfall like delicate ballerinas. Inhaling slowly and deeply, embracing a meditative state, soulful and healing, she strove daily to focus on the positives, the light, the beauty that had evolved and continued to evolve from the ashes of all the unfathomable ugliness that had reared and dominated its evil head since Mother's passing. Adeline's positivity was a work in progress. Difficulty, good and evil tugged simultaneously, with the alternative blackness of her being and the suffering caused in the past lurking ever present just beneath her mind's surface. It was a mindset at which she was working hard at on a daily basis, and a mindset she was determined to eliminate. Trying to make sense of everything she'd learned over the past few months—the struggles, mistakes, deception, greed—had been overwhelming in its entirety, but she had come to learn and, with this knowledge, had accepted that the past could not be changed, edited or expunged. It could only be accepted. *Our past does not have to define us.*

This realisation felt like a lead weight being lifted from her shoulders. Some days were good, some days were not so good, but that was OK. Pappa, her Pappa (the reference brought a smile to her face), King Alif, had a new spring in his step, according to Omar's widow, Helena. 'I've never known Alif to be so happy, it's heart-warming. Heaven knows he's suffered enough,' Helena had murmured in her soft, melodious voice one afternoon, the two of them sipping mint tea in the Butterfly House, located within the Eastern Courtyard. Two strangers getting to know each other.

Pappa had embraced them both, Penelope and Adeline, proudly stating one day with an arm firmly wrapped around each of them, 'I am blessed. Allah, good and mighty, has answered my prayers but doubled the joy by sending me a little bit of my one true love Yasmina and a little bit of the beautiful Betsy who risked all in telling me the truth. I have and always will be forever indebted to those two courageous, independent women.' Tears glistening in his eyes, he'd planted a kiss on the top of both of their heads.

Penelope had moved with Adeline without hesitation, adopting this new country as her own. Her decision had been an easy one, as she didn't want any association with her previous home, or any of her inheritance, instead donating the entirety of it to helping women in domestic violence situations. Pappa had welcomed Penelope unequivocally, for she too had suffered immensely through the chaos of Mother's death confessions; she also has been an innocent victim. The two of them were working through their turbulences together. With all that they'd learnt over the past six months, slowly but indelibly a sense of peace was starting to settle in their heart and souls. They felt like they'd arrived home.

EPILOGUE

Adeline

I'm a true believer in destiny, that fundamentally there's a higher power mapping and guiding our future, our journey, each persons unique. If someone had said to me twelve months before that this time next year I'd be living with my biological father, a father I'd been led to believe my whole life was deceased, in a palace, a princess myself by birth, I would have had serious concerns for their mental health. But here I am. A princess, living in a palace, devoted to and adored by my father. I have been granted this amazing opportunity and am determined to maximise my potential in helping others less fortunate. I've decided to devote my life to helping women who are suffocating under oppressive patriarchal rules in having a voice—*their voice*. The decision was an easy one, my heritage, my journey, leading me to this point of time in my life where it feels right.

I have been gifted a platform as a princess with maximum exposure, the opportunity to incite change, educate viewpoints, ideals, challenge the patriarchal system and gender equality. *Women have a right to make their own choices.* It is time for us all to move forward, together as one, united, equals, without division and prejudice. I've joined forces with a strong, independent, likeminded movement, equally passionate. The waves of change have been in motion for some time here, the modern generation embracing the new-world ideals. The future is looking bright.

AUTHOR'S NOTE

This novel is a work of fiction; however, it does touch on subjects of gender inequality and domestic violence afflicting women globally. I pay homage to the incredible women around the world, both past and present, for their strength of character and commitment in fighting for a more equitable and unified world for the betterment of all.

ABOUT THE AUTHOR

Angela Nagel lives in the picturesque Barossa Valley located in South Australia with her husband James and their cheeky and talkative Sulphur Crested Cockatoo Basil. Three adult children and their partners complete their family. Angela has enjoyed a fulfilling career spanning over four decades helping operate their family owned bakery business. She enjoys travelling, with a particular interest in experiencing different cultures and languages. An avid reader for as long as she can remember, Angela has always held an interest in writing. This is her first novel.